MASTER STORYTELLERS

The Tell-Tale HEART
and other stories by
EDGAR ALLAN POE

Edited, with a biographical
note and a selective bibliography by
Sara Sheldon
Former teacher, Yale-North Haven
Editor, Campus Editions

SCHOLASTIC BOOK SERVICES
New York Toronto London Auckland Sydney Tokyo

Student's Edition: 0-590-08762-2
Teacher's Edition: 0-590-09052-6

Special contents © 1969 by Scholastic Magazines, Inc. All rights reserved.
Published by Scholastic Book Services, a division of Scholastic Magazines, Inc.

15 14 13 12 11 10 9 8 7 6 5   9/7 0 1 2 3/8
Printed in the U.S.A.

CONTENTS

The
Tell-Tale
HEART
and other stories

BIOGRAPHICAL NOTE

Poe's ghost stories are among the most famous in the world — and no wonder. All his life Poe was haunted. Disease and poverty followed him. And there were inner demons as well. For much of his life, Poe feared he was going insane.

Poe's early life reads like a Victorian novel. He was born in 1809 in Boston, Massachusetts, the son of two actors. A year later, his father deserted his mother, who died penniless in the home of a Richmond milliner. Edgar was taken in by John Allan, a well-to-do merchant. Allan was a cold man who took the boy only to please his childless wife.

Lacking affection in Allan's house, Poe sought it in the homes of friends. In particular, he adored the mother of one of his schoolmates, Jane Stith Stanard, who grew mad and died shortly after Poe met her. Poe, desolate, haunted the cemetery at night. (He also wrote the poem "To Helen" in her honor.) Poe's worship of Mrs. Stanard was the first of his many strange passions for women, so intensely experienced yet seldom translated into reality.

In 1826 Allan sent Poe to the University of Virginia. Unfortunately, he gave Poe barely enough money for tuition and no spending money at all. Poe fell in with a wealthy crowd and foolishly tried to make money by gambling. Instead he fell into debt. When Allan refused to pay the debts, Poe left the University and joined the Army. It was a move he instantly regretted, and he wrote to Allan pleading for help. (In those days, the rich could buy their way out of the army by paying for a replacement.) Allan offered to bail Poe out, but only if Poe would accept an appointment to West Point. A year later, Poe deliberately got expelled from the Academy by cutting all drills and classes for a week.

In 1831 Poe went to live with his aunt, Mrs. Clemm, in Baltimore. Mrs. Clemm had a daughter, Virginia, who was later to become Poe's wife. In Baltimore, Poe began writing short stories ("Ms. Found in a Bottle" won first prize in a magazine contest), but he lived on the edge of starvation. He couldn't even accept friendly dinner invitations because his clothes were so shabby.

Poe's fortunes improved slightly when he became editor of a literary magazine in Richmond. He was a brilliant editor who improved the quality of the magazine and greatly increased its circulation. Yet in spite of his relatively secure position, Poe was desperately unhappy. A letter written to a friend shows the intensity of despair for which he cannot name a cause.

You will believe me, when I say that I am still miserable in spite of the great improvement in my circumstances. I am wretched, and know

not why. Console me — for you can. But let it be
quickly — or it will be too late. Write me immediately. Convince me that it is worth one's
while — that it is at all necessary to live.

Alone in a cheap boarding house in Richmond,
Poe feared for his sanity. To relieve the anxiety, he
drank. Poe was a bad drinker. One drink could in-
toxicate him, two could make him rave like a madman, and he seldom stopped at one or two. Because
of these drinking bouts, the owner of the magazine
regretfully (and only temporarily) fired Poe. "Separate
yourself from the bottle and bottle companions forever," he wrote. "No man is safe who drinks before
breakfast."

In 1836 Poe married his cousin Virginia, who was
not quite fourteen at the time. (Or perhaps he
married her secretly the year before.) Many have
speculated on Poe's reason for taking a child bride.
The evidence is that he was passionately in love with
her. When Mrs. Clemm wrote that Virginia might be
sent away to her cousin's to be educated, Poe returned this frantic letter. "It is useless to disguise the
truth that when Virginia goes with Neilson Poe that
I shall never behold her again. Pity me, my dear
Aunty, pity me. Can I calmly resign my life itself? If
she had truly loved me would she not have rejected
the offer with scorn? Oh God have mercy on me!"
The letter apparently did its work. Virginia remained
at home, and a year later became Poe's wife.

From 1839-44, Poe lived in Philadelphia, editing
Burton's Magazine, and its successor, *Graham's.*
These were very productive years for Poe. He wrote
some of his best stories, "The Fall of the House of
Usher" and "The Murders in the Rue Morgue," but
he was still restless and discontent. For one thing, he

was underpaid. For another, he didn't like to take orders. Poe dreamed of a magazine of his own. He chased this chimera for years, in Philadelphia, New York, and Richmond. He left three editorial posts in the hope of realizing it, but the magazine was never to be.

In 1847 Virginia died of tuberculosis. By that time, Poe was so poor he couldn't afford blankets for his wife, and she would have died without bedclothes except for the intercession of a charitable friend. Virginia's long illness wore Poe down, and he floundered about for awhile, seeking a new basis of security. Three women enter the picture here: Helen Whitman, a poet and spiritualist, to whom Poe was briefly engaged; Annie Richmond, a sweet, simple woman with whom Poe was simultaneously in love; and Elmira Royster Shelton, Poe's childhood sweetheart and now a wealthy widow in Richmond. Poe courted Elmira, and perhaps won her consent. A dull lady of position, she seems to have been flattered by the attentions of the notorious romantic poet. In any case, Poe never lived to be married. He drank himself to death in Baltimore, in October 1849, at the age of forty-one.

Sara Sheldon

THE TELL-TALE HEART

TRUE! — nervous — very, very dreadfully nervous I had been and am; but why *will* you say that I am mad? The disease had sharpened my senses — not destroyed — not dulled them. Above all was my sense of hearing acute. I heard all things in the heaven and in the earth. I heard many things in hell. How, then, am I mad? Hearken! and observe how healthily — how calmly I can tell you the whole story.

It is impossible to say how first the idea entered my brain; but once conceived, it haunted me day and night. Object there was none. Passion there was none. I loved the old man. He had never wronged me. He had never given me insult. For his gold I had no desire. I think it was his eye! yes, it was this! One of his eyes resembled that of a vulture — a pale blue eye, with a film over it. Whenever it fell upon me, my blood ran cold; and so by degrees — very gradually — I made up my mind to take the life of the old man, and thus rid myself of the eye forever.

Now this is the point. You fancy me mad. Madmen know nothing. But you should have seen *me*. You should have seen how wisely I proceeded — with what caution — with what foresight — with what dissimulation I went to work! I was never kinder to the old man than during the whole week before I killed him. And every night, about midnight, I turned the latch of his door and opened it — oh, so gently! And then, when I had made an opening sufficient for my head, I put in a dark lantern, all closed, closed, so that no light shone out, and then I thrust in my head. Oh, you would have laughed to see how cunningly I thrust it in! I moved it slowly — very, very slowly, so that I might not disturb the old man's sleep. It took me an hour to place my whole head within the opening so far that I could see him as he lay upon his bed. Ha! — would a madman have been so wise as this? And then, when my head was well in the room, I undid the lantern cautiously — oh, so cautiously — cautiously (for the hinges creaked) — I undid it just so much that a single thin ray fell upon the vulture eye. And this I did for seven long nights — every night just at midnight — but I found the eye always closed; and so it was impossible to do the work; for it was not the old man who vexed me, but his Evil Eye. And every morning, when the day broke, I went boldly into the chamber, and spoke courageously to him, calling him by name in a hearty tone, and inquiring how he had passed the night. So you see he would have been a very profound old man, indeed, to suspect that every night, just at twelve, I looked in upon him while he slept.

Upon the eighth night I was more than usually cautious in opening the door. A watch's minute hand moves more quickly than did mine. Never before that night had I *felt* the extent of my own powers — of my sagacity. I could scarcely contain my feelings of triumph. To think that there I was, opening the door, little by little, and he not even to dream of my secret deeds or thoughts. I fairly chuckled at the idea; and perhaps he heard me; for he moved on the bed suddenly, as if startled. Now you may think that I drew back — but no. His room was as black as pitch with the thick darkness (for the shutters were close fastened, through fear of robbers), and so I knew that he could not see the opening of the door, and I kept pushing it on steadily, steadily.

I had my head in, and was about to open the lantern, when my thumb slipped upon the tin fastening, and the old man sprang up in the bed, crying out — "Who's there?"

I kept quite still and said nothing. For a whole hour I did not move a muscle, and in the meantime I did not hear him lie down. He was still sitting up in the bed listening; just as I have done, night after night, hearkening to the death watches in the wall.

Presently I heard a slight groan, and I knew it was the groan of mortal terror. It was not a groan of pain or of grief — oh, no! — it was the low stifled sound that arises from the bottom of the soul when overcharged with awe. I knew the sound well. Many a night, just at midnight, when all the world slept, it has welled up from my own bosom, deepening, with its dreadful echo, the terrors that distracted me. I say I knew it well. I knew what the old man felt, and pitied him, although I chuckled at heart. I knew that he had been lying awake ever since the first slight noise, when he had turned in the bed. His fears had been ever since growing upon him. He had been trying to fancy them causeless, but could not. He had been saying to himself — "It is nothing but the wind in the chimney — it is only a mouse crossing the floor," or "it is merely a cricket which has made a single chirp." Yes, he had been trying to comfort himself with these suppositions; but he had found all in vain. *All in vain;* because Death, in approaching him, had stalked with his black shadow before him, and enveloped the victim. And it was the mournful influence of the unperceived shadow that caused him to feel — although he neither saw nor heard — to *feel* the presence of my head within the room.

When I had waited a long time, very patiently, without hearing him lie down, I resolved to open a little — a very, very little crevice in the lantern. So I opened it — you cannot imagine how stealthily, stealthily — until, at length, a single dim ray, like the thread of a spider, shot from out the crevice and full upon the vulture eye.

It was open — wide, wide open — and I grew furious as I gazed upon it. I saw it with perfect distinctness — all a dull blue, with a hideous veil over it that chilled the very marrow in my bones; but I could see nothing else of the old man's face or person: I had directed the ray as if by instinct, precisely upon the damned spot.

And now have I not told you that what you mistake for madness is but overacuteness of the senses? — now, I say, there came to my ears a low, dull, quick sound, such as a watch makes when enveloped in cotton. I knew *that* sound well too. It was the beating of the old man's heart. It increased my fury, as the beating of a drum stimulates the soldier into courage.

But even yet I refrained and kept still. I scarcely breathed. I held the lantern motionless. I tried to see how steadily I could maintain the ray upon the eye. Meantime the hellish tattoo of the heart increased. It grew quicker and quicker, and louder and louder every instant. The old man's terror *must* have been extreme!

It grew louder, I say, louder every moment!
— do you mark me well? I have told you that I
am nervous: So I am. And now at the dead hour
of the night, amid the dreadful silence of that
old house, so strange a noise as this excited me
to uncontrollable terror. Yet, for some minutes
longer I refrained and stood still. But the beating grew louder, louder! I thought the heart
must burst. And now a new anxiety seized me —
the sound would be heard by a neighbor! The
old man's hour had come! With a loud yell, I
threw open the lantern and leaped into the
room. He shrieked once — once only. In an instant I dragged him to the floor, and pulled
the heavy bed over him. I then smiled gaily, to
find the deed so far done. But, for many minutes, the heart beat on with a muffled sound.
This, however, did not vex me; it would not be
heard through the wall. At length it ceased. The
old man was dead. I removed the bed and examined the corpse. Yes, he was stone, stone dead.
I placed my hand upon the heart and held it
there many minutes. There was no pulsation.
He was stone dead. His eye would trouble me
no more.

If still you think me mad, you will think so
no longer when I describe the wise precautions
I took for the concealment of the body. The
night waned, and I worked hastily, but in silence. First of all I dismembered the corpse. I
cut off the head and the arms and the legs.

I then took up three planks from the flooring

of the chamber, and deposited all between the scantlings. I then replaced the boards so cleaverly, so cunningly, that no human eye — not even *his* — could have detected anything wrong. There was nothing to wash out — no stain of any kind — no blood spot whatever. I had been too wary for that. A tub had caught all — ha! ha!

When I had made an end of these labors, it was four o'clock — still dark as midnight. As the bell sounded the hour, there came a knocking at the street door. I went down to open it with a light heart — for what had I *now* to fear? There entered three men, who introduced themselves, with perfect suavity, as officers of the police. A shriek had been heard by a neighbor during the night; suspicion of foul play had been aroused; information had been lodged at the police office, and they (the officers) had been deputed to search the premises.

I smiled — for *what* had I to fear? I bade the gentlemen welcome. The shriek, I said, was my own in a dream. The old man, I mentioned, was absent in the country. I took my visitors all over the house. I bade them search — search *well*. I led them, at length, to *his* chamber. I showed them his treasures, secure, undisturbed. In the enthusiasm of my confidence, I brought chairs into the room, and desired them *here* to rest from their fatigues, while I myself, in the wild audacity of my perfect triumph, placed my own seat upon the very spot beneath which reposed the corpse of the victim.

The officers were satisfied. My *manner* had convinced them. I was singularly at ease. They sat, and while I answered cheerily, they chatted familiar things. But, ere long, I felt myself getting pale and wished them gone. My head ached, and I fancied a ringing in my ears, but still they sat and still chatted. The ringing became more distinct — it continued and became more distinct. I talked more freely to get rid of the feeling, but it continued and gained definitiveness — until, at length, I found that the noise was *not* within my ears.

No doubt I now grew *very* pale — but I talked more fluently, and with a heightened voice. Yet the sound increased — and what could I do? It was *a low, dull, quick sound — much such a sound as a watch makes when enveloped in cotton.* I gasped for breath — and yet the officers heard it not. I talked more quickly — more vehemently; but the noise steadily increased. I arose and argued about trifles, in a high key and with violent gesticulations, but the noise steadily increased. Why *would* they not be gone? I paced the floor to and fro with heavy strides, as if excited to fury by the observation of the men — but the noise steadily increased. Oh God! what *could* I do? I foamed — I raved — I swore! I swung the chair upon which I had been sitting, and grated it upon the boards, but the noise arose over all and continually increased. It grew louder — louder — *louder!* And still the men chatted pleasantly, and smiled. Was it possible they heard not? Almighty God! — no, no! They heard! — they suspected! — they *knew!* — they were making a mockery of my horror! — this I thought, and this I think. But anything was better than this agony! Anything was more tolerable than this derision! I could bear those hypocritical smiles no longer! I felt that I must scream or die! — and now — again! — hark! louder! louder! louder! *louder!* —

"Villains!" I shrieked, "dissemble no more! I admit the deed! — tear up the planks! — here, here! — it is the beating of his hideous heart!"

THE MURDERS IN THE
RUE MORGUE

What song the Syrens sang, or what name
Achilles assumed when he hid himself among
women, although puzzling questions, are not
beyond all conjecture.
                              Sir Thomas Browne

THE mental features discoursed of as the analytical, are, in themselves, but little susceptible of analysis. We appreciate them only in
their effects. We know of them, among other
things, that they are always to their possessor,
when inordinately possessed, a source of the
liveliest enjoyment. As the strong man exults
in his physical ability, delighting in such exercises
as call his muscles into action, so glories the analyst in that moral activity which *disentangles*. He
derives pleasure from even the most trivial occupations, bringing his talent into play. He is
fond of enigmas, of conundrums, hieroglyphics;
exhibiting in his solutions of each a degree of
acumen which appears to the ordinary apprehension preternatural. His results, brought

about by the very soul and essence of method, have, in truth, the whole air of intuition.

The faculty of resolution is possibly much invigorated by mathematical study, and especially by that highest branch of it which, unjustly, and merely on account of its retrograde operations, has been called, as if *par excellence*, analysis. Yet to calculate is not in itself to analyze. A chess player, for example, does the one, without effort at the other. It follows that the game of chess, in its effects upon mental character, is greatly misunderstood. I am not now writing a treatise, but simply prefacing a somewhat peculiar narrative by observations very much at random. I will, therefore, take occasion to assert that the higher powers of the reflective intellect are more decidedly and more usefully tasked by the unostentatious game of draughts than by all the elaborate frivolity of chess. In this latter, where the pieces have different and *bizarre* motions, with various and variable values, what is only complex, is mistaken (a not unusual error) for what is profound. The *attention* is here called powerfully into play. If it flag for an instant, an oversight is committed, resulting in injury or defeat. The possible moves being not only manifold, but involute, the chances of such oversights are multiplied; and in nine cases out of ten it is the more concentrative rather than the more acute player who conquers. In draughts, on the contrary, where the moves are *unique* and have but little variation, the probabilities of inadvertence are diminished, and the mere attention being left comparatively unemployed, what advantages are obtained by either party are obtained by superior *acumen*. To be less abstract, let us suppose a game of draughts where the pieces are reduced to four kings, and where, of course, no oversight is to be expected. It is obvious that here the victory can be decided (the players being at all equal) only by some *recherché* [1] movement, the result of some strong exertion of the intellect. Deprived of ordinary resources, the analyst throws himself into the spirit of his opponent, identifies himself therewith, and not unfrequently sees thus, at a glance, the sole methods (sometimes indeed absurdly simple ones) by which he may seduce into error or hurry into miscalculation.

Whist has long been known for its influence upon what is termed the calculating power; and men of the highest order of intellect have been known to take an apparently unaccountable delight in it, while eschewing chess as frivolous. Beyond doubt there is nothing of a similar nature so greatly tasking the faculty of analysis. The best chess player in Christendom *may* be little more than the best player of chess; but proficiency in whist implies capacity for success in all these more important undertakings where mind struggles with mind. When I say profi-

[1] *recherché* — looked for again. (A movement which was perhaps at first missed and then sought again.)

ciency, I mean that perfection in the game which includes a comprehension of *all* the sources whence legitimate advantage may be derived. These are not only manifold, but multiform, and lie frequently among recesses of thought altogether inaccessible to the ordinary understanding. To observe attentively is to remember distinctly; and, so far, the concentrative chess player will do very well at whist; while the rules of Hoyle (themselves based upon the mere mechanism of the game) are sufficiently and generally comprehensible. Thus to have a retentive memory, and proceed by "the book" are points commonly regarded as the sum total of good playing. But it is in matters beyond the limits of mere rule that the skill of the analyst is evinced. He makes, in silence, a host of observations and inferences. So, perhaps, do his companions; and the difference in the extent of the information obtained lies not so much in the validity of the inference as in the quality of the observation. The necessary knowledge is that of *what* to observe. Our player confines himself not at all; nor, because the game is the object, does he reject deductions from things external to the game. He examines the countenance of his partner, comparing it carefully with that of each of his opponents. He considers the mode of assorting the cards in each hand; often counting trump by trump, and honor by honor, through the glances bestowed by their holders upon each. He notes every variation of face as the

play progresses, gathering a fund of thought
from the differences in the expression of cer-
tainty, of surprise, of triumph, or chagrin. From
the manner of gathering up a trick he judges
whether the person taking it can make another
in the suit. He recognizes what is played
through feint, by the manner with which it is
thrown upon the table. A casual or inadvertent
word; the accidental dropping or turning of a
card, with the accompanying anxiety or careless-
ness in regard to its concealment; the counting
of the tricks, with the order of their arrangement; embarrassment, hesitation, eagerness, or
trepidation — all afford, to his apparently intu-
itive perception, indications of the true state of
affairs. The first two or three rounds having
been played, he is in full possession of the contents of each hand, and thenceforward puts
down his cards with as absolute a precision of
purpose as if the rest of the party had turned
outward the faces of their own.

The analytical power should not be confounded with simple ingenuity; for while the
analyst is necessarily ingenious, the ingenious
man is often remarkably incapable of analysis.
The constructive or combining power, by which
ingenuity is usually manifested, and to which
the phrenologists (I believe erroneously) have
assigned a separate organ, supposing it a primitive faculty, has been so frequently seen in those
whose intellect bordered otherwise upon idiocy
as to have attracted general observation among

writers on morals. Between ingenuity and the analytic ability there exists a difference far greater, indeed, than that between the fancy and the imagination, but of a character very strictly analogous. It will be found, in fact, that the ingenious are always fanciful, and the *truly* imaginative never otherwise than analytic.

The narrative which follows will appear to the reader somewhat in the light of a commentary upon the propositions just advanced.

Residing in Paris during the spring and part of the summer of 18 — , I there became acquainted with a Monsieur C. Auguste Dupin. This young gentleman was of an excellent, indeed of an illustrious family, but, by a variety of untoward events, had been reduced to such poverty that the energy of his character succumbed beneath it, and he ceased to bestir himself in the world, or to care for the retrieval of his fortunes. By courtesy of his creditors, there still remained in his possession a small remnant of his patrimony; and, upon the income arising from this, he managed, by means of a rigorous economy, to procure the necessities of life, without troubling himself about its superfluities. Books, indeed, were his sole luxuries, and in Paris these are easily obtained.

Our first meeting was at an obscure library in the Rue Montmartre, where the accident of our both being in search of the same very rare and very remarkable volume brought us into closer communion. We saw each other again and again. I was deeply interested in the little family history which he detailed to me with all that candor which a Frenchman indulges whenever mere self is the theme. I was astonished, too, at the vast extent of his reading; and, above all, I felt my soul enkindled within me by the wild fervor and the vivid freshness of his imagination. Seeking in Paris the objects I then sought, I felt that the society of such a man would be to me a treasure beyond price; and this feeling I frankly confided to him. It was at length arranged that we should live together during my stay in the city; and as my worldly circumstances were somewhat less embarrassed than his own, I was permitted to be at the expense of renting, and furnishing in a style which suited the rather fantastic gloom of our common temper, a time-eaten and grotesque mansion, long deserted through superstitions into which we did not inquire, and tottering to its fall in a retired and desolate portion of the Faubourg St. Germain.

Had the routine of our life at this place been known to the world, we should have been regarded as madmen — although, perhaps, as madmen of a harmless nature. Our seclusion was perfect. We admitted no visitors. Indeed the locality of our retirement had been carefully kept a secret from my own former associates; and it had been many years since Dupin had ceased to know or be known in Paris. We existed unto ourselves alone.

It was a freak of fancy in my friend (for what else shall I call it?) to be enamored of the night for its own sake; and into this *bizarrerie*, as into all his others, I quietly fell; giving myself up to his wild whims with a perfect abandon. The sable [2] divinity would not herself dwell with us always; but we could counterfeit her presence. At the first dawn of the morning we closed all the massy shutters of our old building; lighted a couple of tapers which, strongly perfumed, threw out only the ghastliest and feeblest of rays. By the aid of these we then busied our souls in dreams — reading, writing, or conversing, until warned by the clock of the advent of true Darkness. Then we sallied forth into the streets, arm in arm, continuing the topics of the day, or roaming far and wide until a late hour, seeking, amid the wild lights and shadows of the populous city, that infinity of mental excitement which quiet observation can afford.

At such times I could not help remarking and admiring (although from his rich ideality I had been prepared to expect it) a peculiar analytic ability in Dupin. He seemed, too, to take an eager delight in its exercise — if not exactly in its display — and did not hesitate to confess the pleasure thus derived. He boasted to me, with a low chuckling laugh, that most men, in respect to himself, wore windows in their bosoms, and was wont to follow up such assertions by direct and very startling proofs of his intimate knowledge of my own. His manner at these moments was frigid and abstract; his eyes

[2] sable — black or dark. Here, Poe uses "sable divinity" as he might use Prince of Darkness.

were vacant in expression; while his voice, usually a rich tenor, rose into a treble which would have sounded petulant but for the deliberateness and entire distinctness of the enunciation. Observing him in these moods, I often dwelt meditatively upon the old philosophy of the Bi-Part Soul, and amused myself with the fancy of a double Dupin — the creative and the resolvent.

Let it not be supposed, from what I have just said, that I am detailing any mystery, or penning any romance. What I have described in the Frenchman was merely the result of an excited, or perhaps of a diseased, intelligence. But of the character of his remarks at the periods in question an example will best convey the idea.

We were strolling one night down a long dirty street, in the vicinity of the Palais Royal. Being both, apparently, occupied with thought, neither of us had spoken a syllable for fifteen minutes at least. All at once Dupin broke forth with these words:

"He is a very little fellow, that's true, and would do better for the *Théâtre des Variétés.*"

"There can be no doubt of that," I replied, unwittingly, and not at first observing (so much had I been absorbed in reflection) the extraordinary manner in which the speaker had chimed in with my meditations. In an instant afterward I recollected myself, and my astonishment was profound.

"Dupin," said I, gravely, "this is beyond my comprehension. I do not hesitate to say that I am amazed, and can scarcely credit my senses. How was it possible you should know I was thinking of — ?" Here I paused, to ascertain beyond a doubt whether he really knew of whom I thought.

" — of Chantilly," said he, "why do you pause? You were remarking to yourself that his diminutive figure unfitted him for tragedy."

This was precisely what had formed the subject of my reflections. Chantilly was a *quondam* [3] cobbler of the Rue St. Denis, who, becoming stage-mad, had attempted the role of Xerxes, in Crébillon's tragedy so called, and been notoriously pasquinaded [4] for his pains.

"Tell me, for Heaven's sake," I exclaimed, "the method — if method there is — by which you have been enabled to fathom my soul in this matter." In fact, I was even more startled than I would have been willing to express.

"It was the fruiterer," replied my friend, "who brought you to the conclusion that the mender of soles was not of sufficient height for Xerxes *et id genus omne.*" [5]

"The fruiterer! — you astonish me — I know no fruiterer whomsoever."

"The man who ran up against you as we entered the street — it may have been fifteen minutes ago."

I now remembered that, in fact, a fruiterer,

3 *quondam* — one time, former.
4 pasquinaded — satirized or lampooned.
5 *et id genus omne* — and every one of that kind. (He ·ras too short to play Xerxes, or any noble character like Xerxes.)

carrying upon his head a large basket of apples, had nearly thrown me down, by accident, as we passed from the Rue C—into the thoroughfare where we stood; but what this had to do with Chantilly I could not possibly understand.

There was not a particle of *charlatânerie* about Dupin. "I will explain," he said, "and that you may comprehend all clearly, we will first retrace the course of your meditations, from the moment in which I spoke to you until that of the *rencontre* with the fruiterer in question. The larger links of the chain run thus — Chantilly, Orion, Dr. Nichols, Epicurus, stereotomy,[6] the street stones, the fruiterer."

There are few persons who have not, at some period of their lives, amused themselves in retracing the steps by which particular conclusions of their own minds have been attained. The occupation is often full of interest; and he who attempts it for the first time is astonished by the apparently illimitable distance and incoherence between the starting point and the goal. What, then, must have been my amazement, when I heard the Frenchman speak what he had just spoken, and when I could not help acknowledging that he had spoken the truth. He continued:

"We had been talking of horses, if I remember aright, just before leaving the Rue C—. This was the last subject we discussed. As we crossed into this street, a fruiterer, with a large

6 stereotomy — the art of stone cutting.

basket upon his head, brushing quickiy past us, thrust you upon a pile of paving-stones collected at a spot where the causeway is undergoing repair. You stepped upon one of the loose fragments, slipped, slightly strained your ankle, appeared vexed or sulky, muttered a few words, turned to look at the pile, and then proceeded in silence. I was not particularly attentive to what you did; but observation has become with me, of late, a species of necessity.

"You kept your eyes upon the ground — glancing, with a petulant expression, at the holes and ruts in the pavement (so that I saw you were still thinking of the stones), until we reached the little alley called Lamartine, which has been paved, by way of experiment, with the overlapping and riveted blocks. Here your countenance brightened up, and, perceiving your lips move, I could not doubt that you murmured the word 'stereotomy,' a term very affectedly applied to this species of pavement. I knew that you could not say to yourself 'stereotomy' without being brought to think of atomies, and thus of the theories of Epicurus; and since, when we discussed this subject not very long ago, I mentioned to you how singularly, yet with how little notice, the vague guesses of that noble Greek had met with confirmation in the late nebular cosmogony, I felt that you could not avoid casting your eyes upward to the great nebula in Orion, and I certainly expected that you would do so. You did look up; and I was now assured that I had correctly followed your steps. But in that bitter tirade upon Chantilly, which appeared in yesterday's *Musée,* the satirist, making some disgraceful allusions to the cobbler's change of name upon assuming the buskin, quoted a Latin line about which we have often conversed. I mean the line

Perdidit antiquum litera prima sonum.[7]

I had told you that this was in reference to Orion, formerly written Urion; and, from certain pungencies connected with this explanation, I was aware that you could not have forgotten it. It was clear, therefore, that you would not fail to combine the two ideas of Orion and Chantilly. That you did combine them I saw by the character of the smile which passed over your lips. You thought of the poor cobbler's immolation. So far, you had been stooping in your gait; but now I saw you draw yourself up to your full height. I was then sure that you reflected upon the diminutive figure of Chantilly. At this point I interrupted your meditations to remark that as, in fact, he *was* a very little fellow — that Chantilly — he would do better at the *Théâtre des Variétés.*"

Not long after this, we were looking over an

---

7 *Perdidit antiquum litera prima sonum* — The first letter destroyed the old sound. (The former cobbler, Chantilly, has evidently changed his name, probably by changing the first letter. Dupin compares the change to that in the name of Orion, which used to be spelled Urion.)

evening edition of the *Gazette des Tribunaux,* when the following paragraphs arrested our attention.

"Extraordinary Murders — This morning, about three o'clock, the inhabitants of the Quartier St. Roch were aroused from sleep by a succession of terrific shrieks, issuing, apparently, from the fourth story of a house in the Rue Morgue, known to be in the sole occupancy of one Madame L'Espanaye, and her daughter, Mademoiselle Camille L'Espanaye. After some delay, occasioned by a fruitless attempt to procure admission in the usual manner, the gateway was broken in with a crowbar, and eight or ten of the neighbors entered, accompanied by two gendarmes. By this time the cries had ceased; but, as the party rushed up the first flight of stairs, two or more rough voices in angry contention were distinguished, and seemed to proceed from the upper part of the house. As the second landing was reached, these sounds, also, had ceased, and everything remained perfectly quiet. The party spread themselves, and hurried from room to room. Upon arriving at a large back chamber in the fourth story (the door of which, being found locked, with the key inside, was forced open), a spectacle presented itself which struck everyone present not less with horror than with astonishment.

"The apartment was in the wildest disorder — the furniture broken and thrown about in all directions. There was only one bedstead; and from this the bed had been removed and thrown into the middle of the floor. On a chair lay a razor, besmeared with blood. On the hearth were two or three long and thick tresses of gray human hair, also dabbled with blood, and seeming to have been pulled out by the roots. Upon the floor were found four Napoleons, an earring of topaz, three large silver spoons, three smaller of *métal d' Alger,* and two bags, containing nearly four thousand francs in gold. The drawers of a bureau, which stood in one corner, were open, and had been, apparently, rifled, although many articles still remained in them. A small iron safe was discovered under the bed (not under the bedstead). It was open, with the key still in the door. It had no contents beyond a few old letters and other papers of little consequence.

"Of Madame L'Espanaye no traces were here seen; but an unusual quantity of soot being observed in the fireplace, a search was made in the chimney, and (horrible to relate!) the corpse of the daughter, head downward, was dragged therefrom; it having been thus forced up the narrow aperture for a considerable distance. The body was quite warm. Upon examining it, many excoriations were perceived, no doubt occasioned by the violence with which it had been thrust up and disengaged. Upon the face were many severe scratches and, upon the throat, dark bruises and deep indentations of finger nails, as if the deceased had been throttled to death.

"After a thorough investigation of every portion of the house without further discovery, the party made its way into a small paved yard in the rear of the building, where lay the corpse of the old lady, with her throat so entirely cut that, upon an attempt to raise her, the head fell off. The body, as well as the head, was fearfully mutilated — the former so much so as scarcely to retain any semblance of humanity.

"To this horrible mystery there is not as yet, we believe, the slightest clue."

The next day's paper had these additional particulars:

"*The Tragedy in the Rue Morgue* — Many individuals have been examined in relation to this most extraordinary and frightful affair [the word '*affaire*' had not yet, in France, that levity of import which it conveys with us], but nothing whatever has transpired to throw light upon it. We give below all the material testimony elicited.

"*Pauline Dubourg*, laundress, deposes that she has known both the deceased for three years, having washed for them during that period. The old lady and her daughter seemed on good terms — very affectionate toward each other. They were excellent pay. Could not speak in regard to their mode or means of living. Believes that Madame L. told fortunes for a living. Was reputed to have money put by. Never met any person in the house when she called for the clothes or took them home. Was sure that they had no servant in employ. There appeared to be no furniture in any part of the building except in the fourth story.

"*Pierre Moreau*, tobacconist, deposes that he has been in the habit of selling small quantities of tobacco and snuff to Madame L'Espanaye for nearly four years. Was born in the neighborhood, and has always resided there. The deceased and her daughter had occupied the house in which the corpses were found, for more than six years. It was formerly occupied by a jeweler, who underlet the upper rooms to various persons. The house was the property of Madame L. She became dissatisfied with the abuse of the premises by her tenant, and moved into them herself, refusing to let any portion. The old lady was childish. Witness had seen the daughter some five or six times during the six years. The two lived an exceedingly retired life — were reputed to have money. Had heard it said among the neighbors that Madame L. told fortunes — did not believe it. Had never seen any person enter the door except the old lady and her daughter, a porter once or twice, and a physician some eight or ten times.

"Many other persons, neighbors, gave evidence to the same effect. No one was spoken of as frequenting the house. It was not known whether there were any living connections of Madame L. and her daughter. The shutters of the front windows were seldom opened. Those in the rear were always closed, with the exception of the large back room, fourth story. The house was a good house — not very old.

"*Isidore Musèt*, gendarme, deposes that he was called to the house about three o'clock in the morning, and found some twenty or thirty persons at the gateway, endeavoring to gain admittance. Forced it open, at length, with a bayonet — not with a crowbar. Had but little difficulty in getting it open, on account of its being a double or folding gate, and bolted neither at bottom nor top. The shrieks were continued until the gate was forced — and then suddenly ceased. They seemed to be screams of some person (or persons) in great agony — were loud and drawn out, not short and quick. Witness led the way upstairs. Upon reaching the first landing, heard two voices in loud and angry contention — the one a gruff voice, the other much shriller — a very strange voice. Could distinguish some words of the former, which was that of a Frenchman. Was positive that it was not a woman's voice. Could distinguish the words '*sacré*' and '*diable*.' The shrill voice was that of a foreigner. Could not be sure whether it was the voice of a man or of a woman. Could not make out what was said, but believed the language to be Spanish. The state of the room and of the bodies was described by this witness as we described them yesterday.

"*Henri Duval*, a neighbor, and by trade a silversmith, deposes that he was one of the party who first entered the house. Corroborates the testimony of Musèt in general. As soon as they forced an entrance, they reclosed the door, to keep out the crowd, which collected very fast notwithstanding the lateness of the hour. The shrill voice, this witness thinks, was that of an Italian. Was certain it was not French. Could not be sure that it was a man's voice. It might have been a woman's. Was not acquainted with the Italian language. Could not distinguish the words, but was convinced by the intonation that the speaker was an Italian. Knew Madame L. and her daughter. Had conversed with both frequently. Was sure that the shrill voice was not that of either of the deceased.

" — *Odenheimer*, restauranteur. This witness volunteered his testimony. Not speaking French, was examined through an interpreter. Is a native of Amsterdam. Was passing the house at the time of the shrieks. They lasted for several minutes — probably ten. They were long and loud — very awful and distressing. Was one of those who entered the building. Corroborated the previous evidence in every respect but one. Was sure that the shrill voice was that of a man — of a Frenchman. Could not distinguish the words uttered. They were loud and quick — unequal — spoken apparently in fear as well as in anger. The voice was harsh — not so much shrill as harsh. Could not call it a shrill voice. The gruff voice said repeatedly, '*sacré*,' '*diable*,' and once '*mon Dieu*.'

"*Jules Mignaud*, banker, of the firm of Mignaud et Fils, Rue Deloraine. Is the elder Mignaud. Madame L'Espanaye had some property. Had opened an account with his banking house in the spring of the year (eight years previously). Made frequent deposits in small sums. Had checked for nothing until the third day before her death, when she took out in person the sum of 4000 francs. This sum was paid in gold, and a clerk sent home with the money.

"*Adolphe Le Bon*, clerk to Mignaud et Fils, deposes that on the day in question, about noon, he accompanied Madame L'Espanaye to her residence with the 4000 francs, put up in two bags. Upon the door being opened, Mademoiselle L. appeared and took from his hands one of the bags, while the old lady relieved him of the other. He then bowed and departed. Did not see any person in the street at the time. It is a by-street — very lonely.

"*William Bird*, tailor, deposes that he was one of the party who entered the house. Is an Englishman. Has lived in Paris two years. Was one of the first to ascend the stairs. Heard the voices in contention. The gruff voice was that of a Frenchman. Could make out several words, but cannot now remember all. Heard distinctly '*sacré*' and '*mon Dieu*.' There was a sound at the moment as if of several persons struggling — a scraping and scuffling sound. The shrill voice was very loud — louder than the gruff one. Is sure that it was not the voice of an Englishman. Appeared to be that of a German. Might have been a woman's voice. Does not understand German.

"Four of the above-named witnesses, being recalled, deposed that the door of the chamber in which was found the body of Mademoiselle L. was locked on the inside when the party reached it. Everything was perfectly silent — no groans or noises of any kind. Upon forcing the door no person was seen. The windows, both of the back and front room, were down and firmly fastened from within. A door between the two rooms was closed but not locked. The door leading from the front room into the passage was locked, with the key on the inside. A small room in the front of the house, on the fourth story, at the head of the passage, was open, the door being ajar. This room was crowded with old beds, boxes, and so forth. These were carefully removed and searched. There was not an inch of any portion of the house which was not carefully searched. Sweeps were sent up and down the chimneys. The house is a four-story one, with garrets (mansardes). A trapdoor on the roof was nailed down very securely — did not appear to have been opened for years. The time elapsing between the hearing of the voices in contention and the breaking open of the room door was variously stated by the witnesses. Some made it as short as three minutes — some as long as five. The door was opened with difficulty.

"*Alfonzo Garcio,* undertaker, deposes that he resides in the Rue Morgue. Is a native of Spain. Was one of the party who entered the house. Did not proceed upstairs. Is nervous, and was apprehensive of the consequences of agitation.

Heard the voices in contention. The gruff voice was that of a Frenchman. Could not distinguish what was said. The shrill voice was that of an Englishman — is sure of this. Does not understand the English language, but judges by the intonation.

"*Alberto Montani,* confectioner, deposes that he was among the first to ascend the stairs. Heard the voices in question. The gruff voice was that of a Frenchman. Distinguished several words. The speaker appeared to be expostulating. Could not make out the words of the shrill voice. Spoke quick and unevenly. Thinks it the voice of a Russian. Corroborates the general testimony. Is an Italian. Never conversed with a native of Russia.

"Several witnesses, recalled, here testified that the chimneys of all the rooms on the fourth story were too narrow to admit the passage of a human being. By 'sweeps' were meant cylindrical sweeping-brushes, such as are employed by those who clean chimneys. These brushes were passed up and down every flue in the house. There is no back passage by which any one could have descended while the party proceeded upstairs. The body of Mademoiselle L'Espanaye was so firmly wedged in the chimney that it could not be got down until four or five of the party united their strength.

"*Paul Dumas,* physician, deposes that he was called to view the bodies about daybreak. They were both then lying on the sacking of the bedstead in the chamber where Mademoiselle L.

was found. The corpse of the young lady was much bruised and excoriated. The fact that it had been thrust up the chimney would sufficiently account for these appearances. The throat was greatly chafed. There were several deep scratches just below the chin, together with a series of livid spots which were evidently the impression of fingers. The face was fearfully discolored, and the eyeballs protruded. The tongue had been partially bitten through. A large bruise was discovered upon the pit of the stomach, produced, apparently, by the pressure of a knee. In the opinion of M. Dumas, Mademoiselle L'Espanaye had been throttled to death by some person or persons unknown. The corpse of the mother was horribly mutilated. All the bones of the right leg and arm were more or less shattered. The left tibia much splintered, as well as all the ribs of the left side. Whole body dreadfully bruised and discolored. It was not possible to say how the injuries had been inflicted. A heavy club of wood, or a broad bar of iron — a chair — any large, heavy, and obtuse weapon would have produced such results, if wielded by the hands of a very powerful man. No woman could have inflicted the blows with any weapon. The head of the deceased, when seen by witness, was entirely separated from the body, and was also greatly shattered. The throat had evidently been cut with some very sharp instrument — probably with a razor.

"*Alexandre Etienne,* surgeon, was called with

M. Dumas to view the bodies. Corroborated the testimony, and the opinions of M. Dumas.

"Nothing further of importance was elicited, although several other persons were examined. A murder so mysterious, and so perplexing in all its particulars, was never before committed in Paris — if indeed a murder has been committed at all. The police are entirely at fault — an unusual occurrence in affairs of this nature. There is not, however, the shadow of a clue apparent."

The evening edition of the paper stated that the greatest excitement still continued in the Quartier St. Roch — that the premises in question had been carefully researched, and fresh examinations of witnesses instituted, but all to no purpose. A postscript, however, mentioned that Adolphe Le Bon had been arrested and imprisoned — although nothing appeared to incriminate him beyond the facts already detailed.

Dupin seemed singularly interested in the progress of this affair — at least so I judged from his manner, for he made no comments. It was only after the announcement that Le Bon had been imprisoned, that he asked me my opinion respecting the murders.

I could merely agree with all Paris in considering them an insoluble mystery. I saw no means by which it would be possible to trace the murderer.

"We must not judge of the means," said Dupin, "by this shell of an examination. The

Parisian police, so much extolled for acumen, are cunning, but no more. There is no method in their proceedings, beyond the method of the moment. They make a vast parade of measures; but, not unfrequently, these are so ill-adapted to the objects proposed, as to put us in mind of Monsieur Jourdain's calling for his *robe-de-chambre — pour mieux entendre la musique*.[8] The results attained by them are not unfrequently surprising, but, for the most part, are brought about by simple diligence and activity. When these qualities are unavailing, their schemes fail. Vidocq, for example, was a good guesser, and a persevering man. But, without educated thought, he erred continually by the very intensity of his investigations. He impaired his vision by holding the object too close. He might see, perhaps, one or two points with unusual clearness, but in so doing he, necessarily, lost sight of the matter as a whole. Thus there is such a thing as being too profound. Truth is not always in a well. In fact, as regards the more important knowledge, I do believe that she is invariably superficial. The depth lies in the valleys where we seek her, and not upon the mountaintops where she is found. The modes and sources of this kind of error are well typified in the contemplation of the heavenly bodies. To look at a star by glances — to view it in a sidelong way, by turning toward it the exterior por-

---

[8] *robe-de-chambre — pour mieux entendre la musique —* dressing gown in order to hear the music better.

tions of the retina (more susceptible of feeble impressions of light than the interior), is to behold the star distinctly — is to have the best appreciation of its lustre — a lustre which grows dim just in proportion as we turn our vision *fully* upon it. A greater number of rays actually fall upon the eye in the latter case, but in the former, there is the more refined capacity for comprehension. By undue profundity we perplex and enfeeble thought; and it is possible to make even Venus herself vanish from the firmament by a scrutiny too sustained, too concentrated, or too direct.

"As for these murders, let us enter into some examinations for ourselves, before we make up an opinion respecting them. An inquiry will afford us amusement [I thought this an odd term, so applied, but said nothing] and besides, Le Bon once rendered me a service for which I am not ungrateful. We will go and see the premises with our own eyes. I know G — the Prefect of Police — and shall have no difficulty in obtaining the necessary permission."

The permission was obtained, and we proceeded at once to the Rue Morgue. This is one of those miserable thoroughfares which intervene between the Rue Richelieu and the Rue St. Roch. It was late in the afternoon when we reached it, as this quarter is at a great distance from that in which we resided. The house was readily found; for there were still many persons gazing up at the closed shutters, with an objectless curiosity, from the opposite side of the way.

It was an ordinary Parisian house, with a gateway, on one side of which was a glazed watch-
box, with a sliding panel in the window, indi-
cating a *loge de concierge*. Before going in we
walked up the street, turned down an alley and
then, again turning, passed in the rear of the
building — Dupin, meanwhile, examining the
whole neighborhood, as well as the house, with
a minuteness of attention for which I could see
no possible object.

Retracing our steps we came again to the
front of the dwelling, rang, and, having shown
our credentials, were admitted by the agents in
charge. We went upstairs — into the chamber
where the body of Mademoiselle L'Espanaye
had been found, and where both the deceased
still lay. The disorder of the room had, as usual,
been suffered to exist. I saw nothing beyond
what had been stated in the *Gazette des Tribunaux*. Dupin scrutinized everything — not ex-
cepting the bodies of the victims. We then went
into the other rooms, and into the yard; a gendarme accompanying us throughout. The examination occupied us until dark, when we took
our departure. On our way home my companion stopped in for a moment at the office of
one of the daily papers.

I have said that the whims of my friend were
manifold, and that *je les ménageais*: for this
phrase there is no English equivalent. It was his
humor, now, to decline all conversation on the
subject of the murder, until about noon the next
day. He then asked me, suddenly, if I had ob-

served any thing *peculiar* at the scene of the atrocity.

There was something in his manner of emphasizing the word "peculiar," which caused me to shudder, without knowing why.

"No, nothing *peculiar*," I said, "nothing more, at least, than we both saw stated in the paper."

"The *Gazette*," he replied, "has not entered, I fear, into the unusual horror of the thing. But dismiss the idle opinions of this print. It appears to me that this mystery is considered insoluble, for the very reason which should cause it to be regarded as easy of solution — I mean for the *outré* character of its features. The police are confounded by the seeming absence of motive — not for the murder itself — but for the atrocity of the murder. They are puzzled, too, by the seeming impossibility of reconciling the voices heard in contention, with the facts that no one was discovered upstairs but the assassinated Mademoiselle L'Espanaye, and that there were no means of egress without the notice of the party ascending. The wild disorder of the room; the corpse thrust, with the head downward, up the chimney; the frightful mutilation of the body of the old lady; these considerations, with those just mentioned, and others which I need not mention, have sufficed to paralyze the powers, by putting completely at fault the boasted acumen, of the government agents. They have fallen into the gross but common error of confounding the unusual with the abstruse. But it is by these deviations from the plane of the ordinary, that reason feels its way, if at all, in its search for the true. In investigations such as we are now pursuing, it should not be so much asked 'what has occurred,' as 'what has occurred that has never occurred before.' In fact, the facility with which I shall arrive, or have arrived, at the solution of this mystery, is in the direct ratio of its apparent insolubility in the eyes of the police."

I stared at the speaker in mute astonishment.

"I am now awaiting," continued he, looking toward the door of our apartment, "I am now awaiting a person who, although perhaps not the perpetrator of these butcheries, must have been in some measure implicated in their perpetration. Of the worst portion of the crimes committed, it is probable that he is innocent. I hope that I am right in this supposition; for upon it I build my expectation of reading the entire riddle. I look for the man here — in this room — every moment. It is true that he may not arrive; but the probability is that he will. Should he come, it will be necessary to detain him. Here are pistols; and we both know how to use them when occasion demands their use."

I took the pistols, scarcely knowing what I did, or believing what I heard, while Dupin went on, very much as if in a soliloquy. I have already spoken of his abstract manner at such times. His discourse was addressed to myself; but his voice, although by no means loud, had that intonation which is commonly employed in speaking to someone at a great distance. His eyes, vacant in expression, regarded only the wall.

"That the voices heard in contention," he said, "by the party upon the stairs, were not the voices of the women themselves, was fully proved by the evidence. This relieves us of all doubt upon the question whether the old lady could have first destroyed the daughter, and afterward have committed suicide. I speak of this point chiefly for the sake of method; for the strength of Madame L'Espanaye would have been utterly unequal to the task of thrusting her daughter's corpse up the chimney as it was found; and the nature of the wounds upon her own person entirely precludes the idea of self-destruction. Murder, then, has been committed by some third party; and the voices of this third party were those heard in contention. Let me now advert — not to the whole testimony respecting these voices — but to what was *peculiar* in that testimony. Did you observe anything peculiar about it?"

I remarked that, while all the witnesses agreed in supposing the gruff voice to be that of a Frenchman, there was much disagreement in regard to the shrill, or, as one individual termed it, the harsh voice.

"That was the evidence itself," said Dupin, "but it was not the peculiarity of the evidence. You have observed nothing distinctive. Yet there *was* something to be observed. The witnesses, as you remark, agreed about the gruff voice; they were here unanimous. But in regard to the shrill voice, the peculiarity is — not that they disagreed — but that, while an Italian, an Englishman, a Spaniard, a Hollander, and a Frenchman attempted to describe it, each one spoke of it as that *of a foreigner*. Each is sure that it was not the voice of one of his own countrymen. Each likens it — not to the voice of an individual of any nation with whose language he is conversant — but the converse. The Frenchman supposes it the voice of a Spaniard, and 'might have distinguished some words *had he been acquainted with the Spanish*.' The Dutchman maintains it to have been that of a Frenchman; but we find it stated that '*not understanding French this witness was examined through an interpreter*.' The Englishman thinks it the voice of a German, and '*does not understand German*.' The Spaniard 'is sure' that it was that of an Englishman, but 'judges by the intonation' altogether, '*as he has no knowledge of the English*.' The Italian believes it the voice of a Russian, but '*has never conversed with a native of Russia*.' A second Frenchman differs, moreover, with the first, and is positive that the voice was that of an Italian; but *not being cognizant of that tongue* is, like the Spaniard, 'convinced by the intonation.' Now, how strangely unusual must that voice have really been, about which such testimony as this *could* have been elicited! — in whose *tones*, even denizens of the five great divisions of Europe could recognize nothing familiar! You will say that it might have been the voice of an Asiatic — of an African.

Neither Asiatics nor Africans abound in Paris; but, without denying the inference, I will now merely call your attention to three points. The voice is termed by one witness 'harsh rather than shrill.' It is represented by two others to have been 'quick and *unequal*.' No words — no sounds resembling words — were by any witness mentioned as distinguishable.

"I know not," continued Dupin, "what impression I may have made, so far, upon your own understanding; but I do not hesitate to say that legitimate deductions even from this portion of the testimony — the portion respecting the gruff and shrill voices — are in themselves sufficient to engender a suspicion which should give direction to all farther progress in the investigation of the mystery. I said 'legitimate deductions'; but my meaning is not thus fully expressed. I designed to imply that the deductions are the *sole* proper ones, and that the suspicion arises *inevitably* from them as a single result. What the suspicion is, however, I will not say just yet. I merely wish you to bear in mind that, with myself, it was sufficiently forcible to give a definite form — a certain tendency — to my inquiries in the chamber.

"Let us now transport ourselves, in fancy, to this chamber. What shall we first seek here? The means of egress employed by the murderers. It is not too much to say that neither of us believes in preternatural events. Madame and Mademoiselle L'Espanaye were not destroyed by spirits. The doers of the deed were material and escaped materially. Then how? Fortunately there is but one mode of reasoning upon the point, and that mode *must* lead us to a definite decision. Let us examine, each by each, the possible means of egress. It is clear that the assassins were in the room where Mademoiselle L'Espanaye was found, or at least in the room adjoining, when the party ascended the stairs. It is, then, only from these two apartments that we have to seek issues. The police have laid bare the floors, the ceiling, and the masonry of the walls, in every direction. No *secret* issues could have escaped their vigilance. But, not trusting to *their* eyes, I examined with my own. There were, then, *no* secret issues. Both doors leading from the rooms into the passage were securely locked, with the keys inside. Let us turn to the chimneys. These, although of ordinary width for some eight or ten feet above the hearths, will not admit, throughout their extent, the body of a large cat. The impossibility of egress, by means already stated, being thus absolute, we are reduced to the windows. Through those of the front room no one could have escaped without notice from the crowd in the street. The murderers *must* have passed, then, through those of the back room. Now, brought to this conclusion in so unequivocal a manner as we are, it is not our part, as reasoners, to reject it on account of apparent impossibilities. It is only left for us to prove that these apparent 'impossibilities' are, in reality, not such.

"There are two windows in the chamber. One

of them is unobstructed by furniture, and is wholly visible. The lower portion of the other is hidden from view by the head of the unwieldy bedstead which is thrust close up against it. The former was found securely fastened from within. It resisted the utmost force of those who endeavored to raise it. A large gimlet-hole had been pierced in its frame to the left, and a very stout nail was found fitted therein, nearly to the head. Upon examining the other window, a similar nail was seen similarly fitted in it; and a vigorous attempt to raise this sash failed also. The police were now entirely satisfied that egress had not been in these directions. And, *therefore,* it was thought a matter of supererogation to withdraw the nails and open the windows.

"My own examination was somewhat more particular, and was so for the reason I have just given — because here it was, I knew, that all apparent impossibilities *must* be proved to be not such in reality.

"I proceeded to think thus — a priori. The murderers *did* escape from one of these windows. This being so, they could not have refastened the sashes from the inside, as they were found fastened; the consideration which put a stop, through its obviousness, to the scrutiny of the police in this quarter. Yet the sashes *were* fastened. They *must,* then, have the power of fastening themselves. There was no escape from this conclusion. I stepped to the unobstructed casement, withdrew the nail with some difficulty,

and attempted to raise the sash. It resisted all
my efforts, as I had anticipated. A concealed
spring must, I now knew, exist; and this corro-
boration of my idea convinced me that my
premises, at least, were correct, however mysterious still appeared the circumstances attending
the nails. A careful search soon brought to light
the hidden spring. I pressed it and, satisfied
with the discovery, forbore to raise the sash.

"I now replaced the nail and regarded it attentively. A person passing out through this
window might have reclosed it, and the spring
would have caught — but the nail could not
have been replaced. The conclusion was plain,
and again narrowed the field of my investigations. The assassins *must* have escaped through
the other window. Supposing, then, the springs
upon each sash to be the same, as was probable,
there *must* be found a difference between the
nails, or at least between the modes of their fix-
ture. Getting upon the sacking of the bedstead,
I looked over the headboard minutely at the
second casement. Passing my hand down behind the board, I readily discovered and pressed
the spring, which was, as I had supposed, identical in character with its neighbor. I now looked
at the nail. It was as stout as the other, and apparently fitted in the same manner — driven in
nearly up to the head.

"You will say that I was puzzled; but, if you
think so, you must have misunderstood the
nature of the inductions. To use a sporting
phrase, I had not been once 'at fault.' The scent

had never for an instant been lost. There was no flaw in any link of the chain. I had traced the secret to its ultimate result, and that result was *the nail*. It had, I say, in every respect, the appearance of its fellow in the other window; but this fact was an absolute nullity (conclusive as it might seem to be) when compared with the consideration that here, at this point, terminated the clue. 'There *must* be something wrong,' I said, 'about the nail.' I touched it, and the head, with about a quarter of an inch of the shank, came off in my fingers. The rest of the shank was in the gimlet-hole, where it had been broken off. The fracture was an old one (for its edges were incrusted with rust), and had apparently been accomplished by the blow of a hammer, which had partially imbedded, in the top of the bottom sash, the head portion of the nail. I now carefully replaced this head portion in the indentation whence I had taken it, and the resemblance to a perfect nail was complete — the fissure was invisible. Pressing the spring, I gently raised the sash for a few inches; the head went up with it, remaining firm in its bed. I closed the window, and the semblance of the whole nail was again perfect.

"This riddle, so far, was now unriddled. The assassin had escaped through the window which looked upon the bed. Dropping of its own accord upon his exit (or perhaps purposely closed), it had become fastened by the spring; and it was the retention of this spring which had been mistaken by the police for that of the nail, farther inquiry being thus considered unnecessary.

"The next question is that of the mode of descent. Upon this point I had been satisfied in my walk with you around the building. About five feet and a half from the casement in question there runs a lightning rod. From this rod it would have been impossible for anyone to reach the window itself, to say nothing of entering it. I observed, however, that the shutters of the fourth story were of the peculiar kind called by Parisian carpenters *ferrades* — a kind rarely employed at the present day, but frequently seen upon very old mansions at Lyons and Bordeaux. They are in the form of an ordinary door (a single, not a folding door), except that the lower half is latticed or worked in open trellis — thus affording an excellent hold for the hands. In the present instance these shutters are fully three feet and a half broad. When we saw them from the rear of the house, they were both about half open — that is to say they stood off at right angles from the wall. It is probable that the police, as well as myself, examined the back of the tenement; but, if so, in looking at these *ferrades* in the line of their breadth (as they must have done), they did not perceive this great breadth itself, or, at all events, failed to take it into due consideration. In fact, having once satisfied themselves that no egress could have been made in this quarter, they would naturally bestow here a very cursory examination. It was clear to me, however, that the shutter belonging to the window at the head of the bed, would, if swung fully back to the wall, reach to within two feet of the lightning rod. It was also evident that, by exertion of a very unusual degree of activity and courage, an entrance into the window, from the rod, might have been thus effected. By reaching to the distance of two feet and a half (we now suppose the shutter open to its whole extent) a robber might have taken a firm grasp upon the trelliswork. Letting go, then, his hold upon the rod, placing his feet securely against the wall, and springing boldly from it, he might have swung the shutter so as to close it and, if we imagine the window open at the time, might even have swung himself into the room.

"I wish you to bear especially in mind that I have spoken of a *very* unusual degree of activity as requisite to success in so hazardous and so difficult a feat. It is my design to show you first, that the thing might possibly have been accomplished; but, secondly and *chiefly,* I wish to impress upon your understanding the *very extraordinary* — the almost preternatural character of that agility which could have accomplished it.

"You will say, no doubt, using the language of the law, that 'to make out my case, I should rather undervalue than insist upon a full estimation of the activity required in this matter.' This may be the practice in law, but it is not the usage of reason. My ultimate object is only the truth. My immediate purpose is to lead you to place in juxtaposition, that *very unusual* activity of which I have just spoken, with that

very peculiar shrill (or harsh) and *unequal*
voice, about whose nationality no two persons
could be found to agree, and in whose utterance
no syllabification could be detected."

At these words a vague and half-formed conception of the meaning of Dupin flitted over my
mind. I seemed to be upon the verge of comprehension, without power to comprehend — as
men, at times, find themselves upon the brink
of remembrance, without being able, in the end,
to remember. My friend went on with his discourse.

"You will see," he said, "that I have shifted
the question from the mode of egress to that of
ingress. It was my design to convey the idea that
both were effected in the same manner, at the
same point. Let us now revert to the interior of
the room. Let us survey the appearances here.
The drawers of the bureau, it is said, had been
rifled, although many articles of apparel still remained within them. The conclusion here is
absurd. It is a mere guess — a very silly one —
and no more. How are we to know that the articles found in the drawers were not all these
drawers had originally contained? Madame L'Espanaye and her daughter lived an exceedingly
retired life — saw no company — seldom went
out — had little use for numerous changes of
habiliment. Those found were at least of as good
quality as any likely to be possessed by these
ladies. If a thief had taken any, why did he not
take the best — why did he not take all? In a
word, why did he abandon four thousand francs

in gold to encumber himself with a bundle of linen? The gold *was* abandoned. Nearly the whole sum mentioned by Monsieur Mignaud, the banker, was discovered, in bags, upon the floor. I wish you therefore, to discard from your thoughts the blundering idea of *motive*, engendered in the brains of the police by that portion of the evidence which speaks of money delivered at the door of the house. Coincidences ten times as remarkable as this (the delivery of the money, and murder committed within three days upon the party receiving it), happen to all of us every hour of our lives, without attracting even momentary notice. Coincidences, in general, are great stumbling-blocks in the way of that class of thinkers who have been educated to know nothing of the theory of probabilities — that theory to which the most glorious objects of human research are indebted for the most glorious of illustration. In the present instance, had the gold been gone, the fact of its delivery three days before would have formed something more than a coincidence. It would have been corroborative of this idea of motive. But, under the real circumstances of the case, if we are to suppose gold the motive of this outrage, we must also imagine the perpetrator so vacillating an idiot as to have abandoned his gold and his motive together.

"Keeping now steadily in mind the points to which I have drawn your attention — that peculiar voice, that unusual agility, and that startling absence of motive in a murder so singularly atrocious as this — let us glance at the butchery itself. Here is a woman strangled to death by manual strength, and thrust up a chimney head downward. Ordinary assassins employ no such mode of murder as this. Least of all, do they thus dispose of the murdered. In the manner of thrusting the corpse up the chimney, you will admit that there was something *excessively outré* — something altogether irreconcilable with our common notions of human action, even when we suppose the actors the most depraved of men. Think, too, how great must have been that strength which could have thrust the body *up* such an aperture so forcibly that the united vigor of several persons was found barely sufficient to drag it *down*!

"Turn, now, to other indications of the employment of a vigor most marvelous. On the hearth were thick tresses — very thick tresses — of gray human hair. These had been torn out by the roots. You are aware of the great force necessary in tearing thus from the head even twenty or thirty hairs together. You saw the locks in question as well as myself. Their roots (a hideous sight!) were clotted with fragments of the flesh of the scalp — sure token of the prodigious power which had been exerted in uprooting perhaps half a million hairs at a time. The throat of the old lady was not merely cut, but the head absolutely severed from the body: The instrument was a mere razor. I wish you also to look at the *brutal* ferocity of these deeds. Of the bruises upon the body of Madame L'Espanaye I do not speak. Monsieur Dumas, and his worthy coadjutor Monsieur Etienne, have pronounced that they were inflicted by some obtuse instrument; and so far these gentlemen are very correct. The obtuse instrument was clearly the stone pavement in the yard, upon which the victim had fallen from the window which looked in upon the bed. This idea, however simple it may now seem, escaped the police for the same reason that the breadth of the shutters escaped them — because, by the affair of the nails, their perceptions had been hermetically sealed against the possibility of the windows having ever been opened at all.

"If now, in addition to all these things, you have properly reflected upon the odd disorder of the chamber, we have gone so far as to combine the ideas of an agility astounding, a strength superhuman, a ferocity brutal, a butchery without motive, a *grotesquerie* in horror absolutely alien from humanity, and a voice foreign in tone to the ears of men of many nations, and devoid of all distinct or intelligible syllabification. What result, then, had ensued? What impression have I made upon your fancy?"

I felt a creeping of the flesh as Dupin asked me the question. "A madman," I said, "has done this deed — some raving maniac, escaped from a neighboring *Maison de Santé*." [9]

"In some respects," he replied, "your idea is not irrelevant. But the voices of madmen, even

---

[9] *Maison de Santé* — infirmary, rest home, sanitarium.

in their wildest paroxysms, are never found to
tally with that peculiar voice heard upon the
stairs. Madmen are of some nation, and their
language, however incoherent in its words, has
always the coherence of syllabification. Besides,
the hair of a madman is not such as I now hold
in my hand. I disentangled this little tuft from
the rigidly clutched fingers of Madame L'Espanaye. Tell me what you can make of it."

"Dupin!" I said, completely unnerved, "this
hair is most unusual — this is not *human* hair."

"I have not asserted that it is," said he, "but,
before we decide this point, I wish you to glance
at the little sketch I have here traced upon this
paper. It is a *facsimile* drawing of what has been
described in one portion of the testimony as
'dark bruises and deep indentations of finger
nails' upon the throat of Mademoiselle L'Espanaye, and in another (by Messrs. Dumas and
Etienne) as a 'series of livid spots, evidently the
impression of fingers.'

"You will perceive," continued my friend,
spreading out the paper upon the table before
us, "that this drawing gives the idea of a firm
and fixed hold. There is no *slipping* apparent.
Each finger has retained — possibly until the
death of the victim — the fearful grasp by which
it originally imbedded itself. Attempt, now, to
place all your fingers, at the same time, in the
respective impressions as you see them."

I made the attempt in vain.

"We are possibly not giving this matter a fair
trial," he said. "The paper is spread out upon

a plane surface; but the human throat is cylindrical. Here is a billet of wood, the circumference of which is about that of the throat. Wrap the drawing around it, and try the experiment again."

I did so; but the difficulty was even more obvious than before. "This," I said, "is the mark of no human hand."

"Read now," replied Dupin, "this passage from Cuvier."

It was a minute anatomical and generally descriptive account of the large tawny orangutan of the East Indian Islands. The gigantic stature, the prodigious strength and activity, the wild ferocity, and the imitative propensities of these mammalia are sufficiently well known to all. I understood the full horrors of the murder at once.

"The description of the digits," said I, as I made an end of the reading, "is in exact accordance with this drawing. I see that no animal but an orangutan, of the species here mentioned, could have impressed the identations as you have traced them. This tuft of brownish yellow hair, too, is identical in character with that of the beast of Cuvier. But I cannot possibly comprehend the particulars of this frightful mystery. Besides, there were *two* voices heard in contention, and one of them was unquestionably the voice of a Frenchman."

"True; and you will remember an expression attributed almost unanimously, by the evidence, to this voice, the expression, '*mon Dieu!*' This,

under the circumstances, has been justly characterized by one of the witnesses (Montani, the
confectioner) as an expression of remonstrance
or expostulation. Upon these two words, therefore, I have mainly built my hopes of a full solution of the riddle. A Frenchman was cognizant
of the murder. It is possible — indeed it is far
more than probable — that he was innocent of
all participation in the bloody transactions
which took place. The orangutan may have escaped from him. He may have traced it to the
chamber, but, under the agitating circumstances
which ensued, he could never have recaptured
it. It is still at large. I will not pursue these
guesses — for I have no right to call them more
— since the shades of reflection upon which they
are based are scarcely of sufficient depth to be
appreciable by my own intellect, and since I
could not pretend to make them intelligible to
the understanding of another. We will call
them guesses, then, and speak of them as such.
If the Frenchman in question is indeed, as I
suppose, innocent of this atrocity, this advertisement, which I left last night, upon our return
home, at the office of *Le Monde* (a paper de-
voted to the shipping interest, and much sought
by sailors) , will bring him to our residence."

He handed me a paper, and I read thus:

"CAUGHT — *In the Bois de Boulogne, early in
the morning of the — inst.* (the morning of the
murder), *a very large, tawny orangutan of the
Bornese species. The owner (who is ascertained*

to be a sailor, belonging to a Maltese vessel)
may have the animal again, upon identifying it
satisfactorily, and paying a few charges arising
from its capture and keeping. Call at No. — Rue
—, Faubourg St. Germain — au troisième." [10]

"How was it possible," I asked, "that you
should know the man to be a sailor, and belonging to a Maltese vessel?"

"I do *not* know it," said Dupin. "I am not
sure of it. Here, however, is a small piece of ribbon which, from its form, and from its greasy
appearance, has evidently been used in tying the
hair in one of those long queues of which sailors
are so fond. Moreover, this knot is one which
few besides sailors can tie, and is peculiar to the
Maltese. I picked the ribbon up at the foot of the
lightning rod. It could not have belonged to
either of the deceased. Now if, after all, I am
wrong in my induction from this ribbon, that
the Frenchman was a sailor belonging to a Maltese vessel, still I can have done no harm in saying what I did in the advertisement. If I am in
error, he will merely suppose that I have been
misled by some circumstance into which he will
not take the trouble to inquire. But if I am
right, a great point is gained. Cognizant although innocent of the murder, the Frenchman
will naturally hesitate about replying to the advertisement — about demanding the orangutan.
He will reason thus: 'I am innocent; I am poor;
my orangutan is of great value — to one in my

10 *au troisième* — the third.

circumstance a fortune in itself — why should I lose it through idle apprehensions of danger? Here, it is, within my grasp. It was found in the Bois de Boulogne at a vast distance from the scene of that butchery. How can it ever be suspected that a brute beast should have done the deed? The police are at fault — they have failed to procure the slightest clue. Should they even trace the animal, it would be impossible to prove me cognizant of the murder, or to implicate me in guilt on account of that cognizance. Above all, *I am known*. The advertiser designates me as the possessor of the beast. I am not sure to what limit his knowledge may extend. Should I avoid claiming a property of so great value, which it is known that I possess, I will render the animal, at least, liable to suspicion. It is not my policy to attract attention either to myself or to the beast. I will answer the advertisement, get the orangutan, and keep it close until this matter has blown over.' "

At this moment we heard a step upon the stairs.

"Be ready," said Dupin, "with your pistols, but neither use them nor show them until at a signal from myself."

The front door of the house had been left open, and the visitor had entered, without ringing, and advanced several steps upon the staircase. Now, however, he seemed to hesitate. presently we heard him descending. Dupin was moving quickly to the door, when we again heard him coming up. He did not turn back a second time, but stepped up with decision, and rapped at the door of our chamber.

"Come in," said Dupin, in a cheerful and hearty tone.

A man entered. He was a sailor, evidently, a tall, stout, and muscular looking person, with a certain daredevil expression of countenance, not altogether unprepossessing. His face, greatly sunburnt, was more than half hidden by whisker and mustachio. He had with him a huge oaken cudgel, but appeared to be otherwise unarmed. He bowed awkwardly, and bade us "good evening," in French accents, which, although somewhat Neufchâtelish, were still sufficiently indicative of a Parisian origin.

"Sit down, my friend," said Dupin. "I suppose you have called about the orangutan. Upon my word, I almost envy you the possession of him; a remarkably fine, and no doubt a very valuable animal. How old do you suppose him to be?"

The sailor drew a long breath, with the air of a man relieved of some intolerable burden, and then replied, in an assured tone:

"I have no way of telling — but he can't be more than four or five years old. Have you got him here?"

"Oh, no; we had no conveniences for keeping him here. He is at a livery stable in the Rue Dubourg, just by. You can get him in the morning. Of course you are prepared to identify the property?"

"To be sure I am, sir."

"I shall be sorry to part with him," said Dupin.

"I don't mean that you should be at all this trouble for nothing, sir," said the man. "Couldn't expect it. Am very willing to pay a reward for the finding of the animal — that is to say, anything in reason."

"Well," replied my friend, "that is all very fair, to be sure. Let me think! — what should I have? Oh! I will tell you. My reward shall be this. You shall give me all the information in your power about these murders in the Rue Morgue."

Dupin said the last words in a very low tone, and very quietly. Just as quietly, too, he walked toward the door, locked it, and put the key in his pocket. He then drew a pistol from his bosom and placed it, without the least flurry, upon the table.

The sailor's face flushed up as if he were struggling with suffocation. He started to his feet and grasped his cudgel; but the next moment he fell back into his seat, trembling violently, and with the countenance of death itself. He spoke not a word. I pitied him from the bottom of my heart.

"My friend," said Dupin, in a kind tone, "you are alarming yourself unnecessarily — you are indeed. We mean you no harm whatever. I pledge you the honor of a gentleman, and of a Frenchman, that we intend you no injury. I perfectly well know that you are innocent of the atrocities in the Rue Morgue. It will not do, however, to deny that you are in some measure implicated in them. From what I have already said, you must know that I have had means of information about this matter — means of which you could never have dreamed. Now the thing stands thus. You have done nothing which you could have avoided — nothing, certainly, which renders you culpable. You were not even guilty of robbery, when you might have robbed with impunity. You have nothing to conceal. You have no reason for concealment. On the other hand, you are bound by every principle of honor to confess all you know. An innocent man is now imprisoned, charged with that crime of which you can point out the perpetrator."

The sailor had recovered his presence of mind, in a great measure, while Dupin uttered these words; but his original boldness of bearing was all gone.

"So help me God!" said he, after a brief pause, "I *will* tell you all I know about this affair; but I do not expect you to believe one half I say — I would be a fool indeed if I did. Still, I *am* innocent, and I will make a clean breast if I die for it."

What he stated was, in substance, this. He had lately made a voyage to the Indian Archipelago. A party, of which he formed one, landed at Borneo, and passed into the interior on an excursion of pleasure. Himself and a companion had captured the orangutan. This companion dying, the animal fell into his own exclusive possession. After great trouble, occasioned by the intractable ferocity of his captive during the home voyage, he at length succeeded in lodging it safely at his own residence in Paris, where, not to attract toward himself the unpleasant curiosity of his neighbors, he kept it carefully secluded, until such time as it should recover from a wound in the foot, received from a splinter on board ship. His ultimate design was to sell it.

Returning home from some sailors' frolic on the night, or rather in the morning, of the murder, he found the beast occupying his own bedroom, into which it had broken from a closet adjoining, where it had been, as was thought, securely confined. Razor in hand, and fully lathered, it was sitting before a looking-glass, attempting the operation of shaving, in which it had no doubt previously watched its master through the keyhole of the closet. Terrified at the sight of so dangerous a weapon in the possession of an animal so ferocious, and so well able to use it, the man, for some moments, was at a loss what to do. He had been accustomed, however, to quiet the creature, even in its fiercest moods, by the use of a whip, and to this he now resorted. Upon sight of it, the orangutan sprang at once through the door of the chamber, down the stairs, and thence, through a window, unfortunately open, into the street.

The Frenchman followed in despair; the ape, razor still in hand, occasionally stopped to look back and gesticulate at his pursuer, until the latter had nearly come up with it. It then again made off. In this manner the chase continued for a long time. The streets were profoundly quiet, as it was nearly three o'clock in the morning. In passing down an alley in the rear of the Rue Morgue, the fugitive's attention was arrested by a light gleaming from the open window of Madame L'Espanaye's chamber, in the fourth story of her house. Rushing to the building, it perceived the lightning rod, clambered up with inconceivable agility, grasped the shutter, which was thrown fully back against the wall and, by this means, swung itself directly upon the headboard of the bed. The whole feat did not occupy a minute. The shutter was kicked open again by the orangutan as it entered the room.

The sailor, in the meantime, was both rejoiced and perplexed. He had strong hopes of now recapturing the brute, as it could scarcely escape from the trap into which it had ventured, except by the rod, where it might be intercepted as it came down. On the other hand, there was much cause for anxiety as to what it might do in the house. This latter reflection urged the man still to follow the fugitive. A lightning rod is ascended without difficulty, especially by a sailor, but, when he had arrived as high as the window, which lay far to his left, his career was stopped; the most that he could accomplish was to reach over so as to obtain a glimpse of the interior of the room. At this glimpse he nearly fell from his hold through excess of horror. Now it was that those hideous shrieks arose upon the night, which had startled from slumber the inmates of the Rue Morgue. Madame L'Espanaye and her daughter, habited in their night clothes, had apparently been occupied in arranging some papers in the iron chest already mentioned, which had been wheeled into the middle of the room. It was open, and its contents lay beside it on the floor. The victims must have been sitting with their backs toward the window; and, from the time elapsing between the ingress of the beast and the screams, it seems probable that it was not immediately perceived. The flapping-to of the shutter would naturally have been attributed to the wind.

As the sailor looked in, the gigantic animal had seized Madame L'Espanaye by the hair (which was loose, as she had been combing it), and was flourishing the razor about her face, in imitation of the motions of a barber. The daughter lay prostrate and motionless; she had swooned. The screams and struggles of the old lady (during which the hair was torn from her head) had the effect of changing the probably pacific purposes of the orangutan into those of wrath. With one determined sweep of its muscular arm it nearly severed her head from her body. The sight of blood inflamed its anger into frenzy. Gnashing its teeth, and flashing fire from its eyes, it flew upon the body of the girl, and imbedded its fearful talons in her throat, retaining its grasp until she expired. Its wandering and wild glances fell at this moment upon the head of the bed, over which the face of its master, rigid with horror, was just discernible. The fury of the beast, who no doubt bore still in mind the dreaded whip, was instantly converted into fear. Conscious of having deserved punishment, it seemed desirous of concealing its bloody deeds, and skipped about the chamber in an agony of nervous agitation; throwing down and breaking the furniture as it moved, and dragging the bed from the bedstead. In conclusion, it seized first the corpse of the daughter, and thrust it up the chimney, as it was found; then that of the old lady, which it immediately hurled through the window headlong.

As the ape approached the casement with its mutilated burden, the sailor shrank aghast to the rod and, rather gliding than clambering down it, hurried at once home — dreading the consequences of the butchery, and gladly abandoning, in his terror, all solicitude about the fate of the orangutan. The words heard by the party upon the staircase were the Frenchman's exclamations of horror and affright, commingled with the fiendish jabberings of the brute.

I have scarcely anything to add. The orangutan must have escaped from the chamber, by the rod, just before the breaking of the door. It must have closed the window as it passed through it. It was subsequently caught by the owner himself, who obtained for it a very large sum at the Jardin des Plantes.[11] Le Bon was in-

11 Jardin des Plantes — located in Paris, it is one of the earliest (c. 1732) official zoological gardens.

stantly released, upon our narration of the circumstances (with some comments from Dupin) at the bureau of the Prefect of Police. This functionary, however well disposed to my friend, could not altogether conceal his chagrin at the turn which affairs had taken, and was fain to indulge in a sarcasm or two about the propriety of every person minding his own business.

"Let him talk," said Dupin, who had not thought it necessary to reply. "Let him discourse; it will ease his conscience. I am satisfied with having defeated him in his own castle. Nevertheless, that he failed in the solution of this mystery, is by no means that matter for wonder which he supposes it; for, in truth, our friend the Prefect is somewhat too cunning to be profound. In his wisdom is no *stamen*. It is all head and no body, like the pictures of the Goddess Laverna — or, at best, all head and shoulders, like a codfish. But he is a good creature after all. I like him especially for one master stroke of cant, by which he has attained his reputation for ingenuity. I mean the way he has '*de nier ce qui est, et d'expliquer ce qui n'est pas*'." [12]

12 *de nier ce qui est, et d'expliquer ce qui n'est pas* — To deny that which is, and to explain that which is not.

Ms.
FOUND
IN A BOTTLE

Qui n'a plus qu'un moment à vivre
N'a plus rien à dissimuler.[13]
— *Quinault — Atys*

O<small>F</small> my country and of my family I have little
to say. Ill-usage and length of years have
driven me from the one and estranged me from
the other. Hereditary wealth afforded me an
education of no common order, and a contem-
plative turn of mind enabled me to methodize
the stories which early study diligently garnered
up. Beyond all things, the works of the German
moralists gave me great delight; not from my ill-
advised admiration of their eloquent madness,
but from the ease with which my habits of rigid
thought enabled me to detect their falsities. I
have often been reproached with the aridity of
my genius; a deficiency of imagination has been

---

13 *Qui n'a plus qu'un moment à vivre / N'a plus rien à
dissimuler* — He who has no more than a moment to live,
has nothing left to hide.

imputed to me as a crime; and the *Pyrrhonism* [14] of my opinions has at all times rendered me notorious. Indeed, a strong relish for physical philosophy has, I fear, tinctured my mind with a very common error of this age — I mean the habit of referring occurrences, even the least susceptible of such reference, to the principles of that science. Upon the whole, no person could be less liable than myself to be led away from the severe precincts of truth by the *ignes fatui* [15] of superstition. I have thought proper to premise thus much, lest the incredible tale I have to tell should be considered rather the raving of a crude imagination than the positive experience of a mind to which the reveries of fancy have been a dead letter and a nullity.

After many years spent in foreign travel, I sailed in the year 18— from the port of Batavia, in the rich and populous island of Java, on a voyage to the Archipelago Islands. I went as passenger, having no other inducement than a kind of nervous restlessness which haunted me as a fiend.

Our vessel was a beautiful ship of about four hundred tons, copper-fastened, and built at Bombay of Malabar teak. She was freighted with cotton wool and oil, from the Lachadive Islands. We had also on board coir, jaggeree,

14 Pyrrhonism — the philosophical doctrines of skepticism; name taken from Pyrrho, a 4th century B.C. Greek philosopher who founded the movement.
15 *ignes fatui* — false lights, will-o'-the-wisps. (Something illusory.)

ghee,[16] coconuts, and a few cases of opium. The stowage was clumsily done, and the vessel consequently crank.[17]

We got underway with a mere breath of wind, and for many days stood along the eastern coast of Java, without an incident to beguile the monotony of our course other than the occasional meeting with some of the small grabs [18] of the Archipelago to which we were bound.

One evening, leaning over the taffrail, I observed a very singular isolated cloud, to the Northwest. It was remarkable, as well from its color as from its being the first we had seen since our departure from Batavia. I watched it attentively until sunset, when it spread all at once to the eastward and westward, girting in the horizon with a narrow strip of vapor, and looking like a long line of low beach. My notice was soon afterward attracted by the dusky-red appearance of the moon and the peculiar character of the sea. The latter was undergoing a rapid change, and the water seemed more than usually transparent. Although I could distinctly see the bottom, yet, heaving the lead, I found the ship in fifteen fathoms. The air now became intolerably hot, and was loaded with spiral exhalations similar to those arising from heated iron. As night came on, every breath of wind died away, and a more entire calm it is impos-

16 coir, jaggeree, ghee — rope, brown sugar, butter.
17 crank — out of kilter, easily tipped.
18 grabs — Oriental coasting ships, usually having two masts and a triangular shaped sail.

sible to conceive. The flame of a candle burned upon the poop without the least perceptible motion, and a long hair, held between the finger and thumb, hung without the possibility of detecting a vibration. However, as the captain said he could perceive no indication of danger, and as we were drifting in bodily to shore, he ordered the sails to be furled and the anchor let go. No watch was set, and the crew, consisting principally of Malays, stretched themselves deliberately upon deck. I went below — not without a full presentiment of evil. Indeed, every appearance warranted me in apprehending a simoon. I told the captain of my fears; but he paid no attention to what I said, and left me without deigning to give a reply. My uneasiness, however, prevented me from sleeping, and about midnight I went upon deck. As I placed my foot upon the upper step of the companion ladder, I was startled by a loud, humming noise, like that occasioned by the rapid revolution of a mill wheel, and before I could ascertain its meaning, I found the ship quivering to its center. In the next instant a wilderness of foam hurled us upon our beam ends, and, rushing over us fore and aft, swept the entire deck from stem to stern.

The extreme fury of the blast proved, in a great measure, the salvation of the ship. Although completely waterlogged, yet, as her masts had gone by the board, she rose, after a minute, heavily from the sea, and, staggering awhile beneath the immense pressure of the tempest, finally righted.

By what miracle I escaped destruction, it is impossible to say. Stunned by the shock of the water, I found myself, upon recovery, jammed in between the stern post and rudder. With great difficulty I regained my feet and, looking dizzily around, was at first struck with the idea of our being among breakers; so terrific, beyond the wildest imagination, was the whirlpool of mountainous and foaming ocean within which we were engulfed. After awhile I heard the voice of an old Swede, who had shipped with us at the moment of leaving port. I hallooed to him with all my strength, and presently he came reeling aft. We soon discovered that we were the sole survivors of the accident. All on deck, with the exception of ourselves, had been swept overboard; the captain and mates must have perished while they slept, for the cabins were deluged with water. Without assistance we could expect to do little for the security of the ship, and our exertions were at first paralyzed by the momentary expectation of going down. Our cable had, of course, parted like pack thread, at the first breath of the hurricane, or we should have been instantaneously overwhelmed. We scudded with frightful velocity before the sea, and the water made clear breaches over us. The framework of our stern was shattered excessively, and, in almost every respect, we had received considerable injury; but to our extreme joy we found the pumps unchoked, and that we had made no great shifting of our ballast. The main fury of the blast had already blown over, and we apprehended little danger from the violence of the wind; but we looked forward to its total cessation with dismay, well believing that, in our shattered condition, we should inevitably perish in the tremendous swell which would ensue. But this very just apprehension seemed by no means likely to be soon verified. For five entire days and nights — during which our only subsistence was a small quantity of jaggeree, procured with great difficulty from the forecastle — the hulk flew at a rate defying computation, before rapidly succeeding flaws of wind, which, without equaling the first violence of the simoon, were still more terrific than any tempest I had before encountered. Our course for the first four days was, with trifling variations, southeast and by south; and we must have run down the coast of New Holland. On the fifth day the cold became extreme, although the wind had hauled round a point more to the northward. The sun arose with a sickly yellow luster, and clambered a very few degrees above the horizon, emitting no decisive light. There were no clouds apparent, yet the wind was upon the increase, and blew with a fitful and unsteady fury. About noon, as nearly as we could guess, our attention was again arrested by the appearance of the sun. It gave out no light, properly so called, but a dull and sullen glow without reflection, as if all its rays were polarized. Just before sinking within the turgid sea, its central fires suddenly went out, as if hurriedly extinguished by some unaccountable power. It was a dim, silverlike rim, alone, as it rushed down the unfathomable ocean.

We waited in vain for the arrival of the sixth day — that day to me has not yet arrived — to the Swede never did arrive. Thenceforward we were enshrouded in pitchy darkness, so that we could not have seen an object at twenty paces from the ship. Eternal night continued to envelop us, all unrelieved by the phosphoric sea brilliancy to which we had been accustomed in the tropics. We observed, too, that, although the tempest continued to rage with unabated violence, there was no longer to be discovered the usual appearance of surf, or foam, which had hitherto attended us. All around were horror, and thick gloom, and a black sweltering desert of ebony. Superstitious terror crept by degrees into the spirit of the old Swede, and my own soul was wrapt in silent wonder. We neglected all care of the ship, as worse than useless, and securing ourselves as well as possible to the stump of the mizenmast, looked out bitterly into the world of ocean. We had no means of calculating time, nor could we form any guess of our situation. We were, however, well aware of having made farther to the southward than any previous navigators, and felt great amazement at not meeting with the usual impediments of ice. In the meantime every moment threatened to be our last — every mountainous billow hurried to overwhelm us. The swell surpassed anything I had imagined possible, and that we were not instantly buried is a miracle. My companion spoke of the lightness of our cargo, and reminded me of the excellent qualities of our ship; but I could not help feeling the utter hopelessness of hope itself, and prepared myself gloomily for that death which I thought nothing could defer beyond an hour, as, with every knot of way the ship made, the swelling of the black stupendous seas became more dismally appalling. At times we gasped for breath at an elevation beyond the albatross — at times became dizzy with the velocity of our descent into some watery hell, where the air grew stagnant, and no sound disturbed the slumbers of the kraken.[19]

We were at the bottom of one of these abysses when a quick scream from my companion broke fearfully upon the night. "See! see! see!" As he spoke, I became aware of a dull sullen glare of red light which streamed down the sides of the vast chasm where we lay and threw a fitful brilliancy upon our deck. Casting my eyes upwards, I beheld a spectacle which froze the current of my blood. At a terrific height directly above us, and upon the very verge of the precipitous descent, hovered a gigantic ship of perhaps four thousand tons. Although upreared upon the summit of a wave more than a hundred times her own altitude, her apparent size still exceeded that of any ship of the line or East Indianman in existence. Her huge hull was of a deep dingy black, unrelieved by any of the customary carvings of a ship. A single row of brass

19 kraken — a Scandinavian sea monster; probably arising from the chance sightings of giant squids.

cannon portruded from her open ports, and dashed from the polished surface the fires of innumerable battle lanterns which swung to and fro about her rigging. But what mainly inspired us with horror and astonishment was that she bore up under a press of sail in the very teeth of that supernatural sea and of that ungovernable hurricane. When we first discovered her, her bows were alone to be seen, as she rose slowly from the dim and horrible gulf beyond her. For a moment of intense terror she paused upon the giddy pinnacle as if in contemplation of her own sublimity, then trembled, and tottered, and — came down.

At this instant, I know not what sudden self-possession came over my spirit. Staggering as far aft as I could, I awaited fearlessly the ruin that was to overwhelm. Our own vessel was at length ceasing from her struggles, and sinking with her head to the sea. The shock of the descending mass struck her, consequently, in that portion of her frame which was nearly under water, and the inevitable result was to hurl me, with irresistible violence, upon the rigging of the stranger.

As I fell, the ship hove in stays and went about; and to the confusion ensuing I attributed my escape from the notice of the crew. With little difficulty I made my way, unperceived, to the main hatchway, which was partially open, and soon found an opportunity of secreting myself in the hold. Why I did so I can hardly tell. An indefinite sense of awe, which at first sight of the navigators of the ship had taken hold of my mind, was perhaps the principle of my concealment. I was unwilling to trust myself with a race of people who had offered, to the cursory glance I had taken, so many points of vague novelty, doubt, and apprehension. I therefore thought proper to contrive a hiding place in the hold. This I did by removing a small portion of the shifting boards, in such a manner as to afford me a convenient retreat between the huge timbers of the ship.

I had scarcely completed my work when a footstep in the hold forced me to make use of it. A man passed by my place of concealment with a feeble and unsteady gait. I could not see his face, but had an opportunity of observing his general appearance. There was about it an evidence of great age and infirmity. His knees tottered beneath a load of years, and his entire frame quivered under the burden. He muttered to himself in a low broken tone, some words of a language which I could not understand, and groped in a corner among a pile of singular-looking instruments and decayed charts of navigation. His manner was a wild mixture of the peevishness of second childhood, and the solemn dignity of a God. He at length went on deck, and I saw him no more.

A feeling for which I have no name has taken possession of my soul — a sensation which will admit of no analysis, to which the lessons of by-gone time are inadequate, and for which I fear futurity itself will offer me no key. To a mind constituted like my own, the latter consideration is an evil. I shall never — I know that I shall never — be satisfied with regard to the nature of my conceptions. Yet it is not wonderful that these conceptions are indefinite, since they have their origin in sources so utterly novel. A new sense — a new entity is added to my soul.

It is long since I first trod the deck of this terrible ship, and the rays of my destiny are, I think, gathering to a focus. Incomprehensible men! Wrapped up in meditations of a kind which I cannot divine, they pass me by unnoticed. Concealment is utter folly on my part, for the people *will not* see. It is but just now that I passed directly before the eyes of the mate; it was no long while ago that I ventured into the captain's own private cabin, and took thence the materials with which I write and have written. I shall from time to time continue this journal. It is true that I may not find an opportunity of transmitting it to the world, but I will not fail to make the endeavor. At the last moment I will enclose the ms. in a bottle and cast it within the sea.

An incident has occurred which has given me new room for meditation. Are such things the operation of ungoverned chance? I had ventured upon deck and thrown myself down, without attracting any notice, among a pile of ratlin stuff and old sails, in the bottom of the yawl.

While musing upon the singularity of my fate, I unwittingly daubed with a tar brush the edges of a neatly folded studding sail which lay near me on a barrel. The studding sail is now bent upon the ship, and the thoughtless touches of the brush are spread out into the word Dis-covery.

I have made my observations lately upon the structure of the vessel. Although well armed, she is not, I think, a ship of war. Her rigging, build, and general equipment, all negate a supposition of this kind. What she *is not,* I can easily per-ceive; what she *is,* I fear it is impossible to say. I know not how it is, but in scrutinizing her strange model and singular cast of spars, her huge size and overgrown suits of canvas, her severely simple bow and antiquated stern, there will occasionally flash across my mind a sensa-tion of familiar things, and there is always mixed up with such indistinct shadows of recol-lection, an unaccountable memory of old for-eign chronicles and ages long ago.

I have been looking at the timbers of the ship She is built of a material to which I am a stran-ger. There is a peculiar character about the wood which strikes me as rendering it unfit for the purpose to which it has been applied. I mean its extreme *porousness,* considered inde-pendently of the worm-eaten condition which is a consequence of navigation in these seas and apart from the rottenness attendant upon age. It will appear perhaps an observation somewhat

overcurious, but this would have every characteristic of Spanish oak, if Spanish oak were dis-
tended by any unnatural means.

In reading the above sentence, a curious
apothegm of an old weather-beaten Dutch navi-
gator comes full upon my recollection. "It is as
sure," he was wont to say, when any doubt was
entertained of his veracity, "as sure as there is a
sea where the ship itself will grow in bulk like
the living body of the seaman."

About an hour ago, I made bold to trust myself among a group of the crew. They paid me
no manner of attention and, although I stood
in the very midst of them all, seemed utterly unconscious of my presence. Like the one I had at
first seen in the hold, they all bore about them
the marks of a hoary old age. Their knees trembled with infirmity; their shoulders were bent
double with decrepitude; their shriveled skins
rattled in the wind; their voices were low, tremulous, and broken; their eyes glistened with the
rheum of years; and their gray hairs streamed
terribly in the tempest. Around them, on every
part of the desk, lay scattered mathematical instruments of the most quaint and obsolete con-
struction.

I mentioned some time ago, the bending of a
studding sail. From that period, the ship, being
thrown dead off the wind, has continued her
terrific course due south, with every rag of can-

vas packed upon her, from her truck to her lower studding-sail booms, and rolling every moment her top-gallant yardarms into the most appalling hell of water which it can enter into the mind of man to imagine. I have just left the deck, where I find it impossible to maintain a footing, although the crew seem to experience little inconvenience. It appears to me a miracle of miracles that our enormous bulk is not swallowed up at once and forever. We are surely doomed to hover continually upon the brink of eternity, without taking a final plunge into the abyss. From billows a thousand times more stupendous than any I have ever seen, we glide away with the facility of the arrowy sea gull; and the colossal waters rear their heads above us like demons of the deep, but like demons confined to simple threats, and forbidden to destroy. I am led to attribute these frequent escapes to the only natural cause which can account for such effect. I must suppose the ship to be within the influence of some strong current, or impetuous undertow.

I have seen the captain face to face, and in his own cabin — but, as I expected, he paid me no attention. Although in his appearance there is, to a casual observer, nothing which might bespeak him more or less than man, still, a feeling of irrepressible reverence and awe mingled with the sensation of wonder with which I regarded him. In stature, he is nearly my own height; that is, about five feet eight inches. He is of a well-

knit and compact frame of body, neither robust
nor remarkable otherwise. But it is the singularity of the expression which reigns upon the face
— it is the intense, the wonderful, the thrilling
evidence of old age so utter, so extreme, which
excites within my spirit a sense, a sentiment
ineffable. His forehead, although little wrin-
kled, seems to bear upon it the stamp of a myr-
iad years. His gray hairs are records of the past,
and his grayer eyes are sybils [20] of the future. The
cabin floor was thickly strewn with strange, iron-
clasped folios, and moldering instruments of
science, and obsolete long-forgotten charts. His
head was bowed down upon his hands, and he
pored, with a fiery, unquiet eye, over a paper
which I took to be a commission, and which, at
all events, bore the signature of a monarch. He
murmured to himself — as did the first seaman
whom I saw in the hold — some low peevish
syllables of a foreign tongue; and although the
speaker was close at my elbow, his voice seemed
to reach my ears from the distance of a mile.

The ship and all in it are imbued with the
spirit of Eld. The crew glide to and fro like the
ghosts of buried centuries; their eyes have an
eager and uneasy meaning; and when their
figures fall athwart my path in the wild glare
of the battle lanterns, I feel as I have never felt
before, although I have been all my life a dealer

20 sybils — any one of several prophetesses of the ancient
world; the name has become synonymous with fortune
teller.

in antiquities, and have imbibed the shadows of fallen columns at Balbec, and Tadmor, and Persepolis, until my very soul has become a ruin.

When I look around me, I feel ashamed of my former apprehension. If I tremble at the blast which has hitherto attended us, shall I not stand aghast at a warring of wind and ocean, to convey any idea of which, the words tornado and simoon are trivial and ineffective? All in the immediate vicinity of the ship is the blackness of eternal night, and a chaos of foamless water; but, about a league on either side of us, may be seen, indistinctly and at intervals, stupendous ramparts of ice, towering away into the desolate sky, and looking like the walls of the universe.

As I imagined, the ship proves to be in a current — if that appellation can properly be given to a tide which, howling and shrieking by the white ice, thunders on the southward with a velocity like the headlong dashing of a cataract.

To conceive the horror of my sensations is, I presume, utterly impossible; yet a curiosity to penetrate the mysteries of these awful regions predominates even over my despair, and will reconcile me to the most hideous aspect of death. It is evident that we are hurrying onward to some exciting knowledge — some never-to-be-imparted secret, whose attainment is destruction. Perhaps this current leads us to the southern pole itself. It must be confessed that a supposition apparently so wild has every probability in its favor.

The crew pace the deck with unquiet and tremulous step; but there is upon their countenance an expression more of the eagerness of hope than of the apathy of despair.

In the meantime the wind is still in our poop and, as we carry a crowd of canvas, the ship is at times lifted bodily from out the sea! Oh, horror upon horror! — the ice opens suddenly to the right, and to the left, and we are whirling dizzily, in immense concentric circles, round and round the borders of a gigantic amphitheatre, the summit of whose walls is lost in the darkness and the distance. But little time will be left me to ponder upon my destiny! The circles rapidly grow small — we are plunging madly within the grasp of the whirlpool — and amid a roaring, and bellowing, and thundering of ocean and tempest, the ship is quivering — oh God! and — going down!

Note: The "Ms. Found in a Bottle," was originally published in 1831, and it was not until many years afterward that I became acquainted with the maps of Mercator, in which the ocean is represented as rushing, by four mouths into the (northern) polar gulf, to be absorbed into the bowels of the earth; the pole itself being represented by a black rock, towering to a prodigious height.

THE CASK OF AMONTILLADO

THE thousand injuries of Fortunato I had borne as I best could; but when he ventured upon insult, I vowed revenge. You, who so well know the nature of my soul, will not suppose, however, that I gave utterance to a threat. *At length* I would be avenged; this was a point definitely settled — but the very definitiveness with which it was resolved precluded the idea of risk. I must not only punish, but punish with impunity. A wrong is unredressed when retribution overtakes its redresser. It is equally unredressed when the avenger fails to make himself felt as such to him who has done the wrong.

It must be understood that neither by word nor deed had I given Fortunato cause to doubt my goodwill. I continued, as was my wont, to smile in his face, and he did not perceive that my smile *now* was at the thought of his immolation.

He had a weak point — this Fortunato — although in other regards he was a man to be respected and even feared. He prided himself on his connoisseurship in wine. Few Italians have the true virtuoso spirit. For the most part their enthusiasm is adopted to suit the time and opportunity — to practice imposture upon the British and Austrian *millionaires*. In painting and gemmary, Fortunato, like his countrymen, was a quack, but in the matter of old wines he was sincere. In this respect I did not differ from him materially: I was skillful in the Italian vintages myself, and bought largely whenever I could.

It was about dusk, one evening during the supreme madness of the carnival season, that I encountered my friend. He accosted me with excessive warmth, for he had been drinking much. The man wore motley. He had on a tight-fitting partistriped dress, and his head was surmounted by the conical cap and bells. I was so pleased to see him that I thought I should never have done wringing his hand.

I said to him: "My dear Fortunato, you are luckily met. How remarkably well you are looking today! But I have received a pipe of what passes for Amontillado, and I have my doubts."

"How?" said he. "Amontillado? A pipe? Impossible! And in the middle of the carnival!"

"I have my doubts," I replied, "and I was silly enough to pay the full Amontillado price without consulting you in the matter. You were not to be found and I was fearful of losing a bargain."

"Amontillado!"

"I have my doubts."

"Amontillado!

"And I must satisfy them."

"Amontillado!"

"As you are engaged, I am on my way to Luchesi. If anyone has a critical turn, it is he. He will tell me — "

"Luchesi cannot tell Amontillado from Sherry."

"And yet some fools will have it that his taste is a match for your own."

"Come, let us go."

"Whither?"

"To your vaults."

"My friend, no; I will not impose upon your good nature. I perceive you have an engagement. Luchesi — "

"I have no engagement — come."

"My friend, no. It is not the engagement, but the severe cold with which I perceive you are afflicted. The vaults are insufferably damp. They are encrusted with niter." [21]

"Let us go, nevertheless. The cold is merely nothing. Amontillado! You have been imposed

21 niter — potassium or sodium nitrate; niter usually refers to a substance which is diffused through the air.

upon. And as for Luchesi, he cannot distinguish
Sherry from Amontillado."

Thus speaking, Fortunato possessed himself
of my arm. Putting on a mask of black silk, and
drawing a *roquelaire* [22] closely about my person,
I suffered him to hurry me to my palazzo.

There were no attendants at home; they had
absconded to make merry in honor of the time.
I had told them that I should not return until
the morning, and had given them explicit orders not to stir from the house. These orders
were sufficient, I well knew, to insure their immediate disappearance, one and all, as soon as
my back was turned.

I took from their sconces two flambeaux, and
giving one to Fortunato, bowed him through
several suites of rooms to the archway that led
into the vaults. I passed down a long and winding staircase, requesting him to be cautious as
he followed. We came at length to the foot of
the descent, and stood together on the damp
ground of the catacombs of the Montresors.

The gait of my friend was unsteady, and the
bells upon his cap jingled as he strode.

"The pipe?" said he.

"It is farther on," said I, "but observe the
white webwork which gleams from these cavern
walls."

He turned toward me, and looked into my
eyes with two filmy orbs that distilled the rheum
of intoxication.

22 *roquelaire* — a long coat, tight at the waist, formerly
worn by Frenchmen.

"Niter?" he asked, at length.

"Niter," I replied. "How long have you had that cough?"

"Ugh! ugh! ugh! — ugh! ugh! ugh! — ugh! ugh! ugh! — ugh! ugh! ugh! — ugh! ugh! ugh!"

My poor friend found it impossible to reply for many minutes.

"It is nothing," he said, at last.

"Come," I said, with decision, "we will go back, your health is precious. You are rich, respected, admired, beloved; you are happy, as once I was. You are a man to be missed. For me it is no matter. We will go back; you will be ill and I cannot be responsible. Besides, there is Luchesi — "

"Enough," he said, "the cough is a mere nothing; it will not kill me. I shall not die of a cough."

"True — true," I replied, "and, indeed, I had no intention of alarming you unnecessarily, but you should use all proper caution. A draught of this Médoc will defend us from the damp."

Here I knocked off the neck of bottle which I drew from a long row of its fellows that lay upon the mould.

"Drink," I said, presenting him the wine.

He raised it to his lips with a leer. He paused and nodded to me familiarly, while his bells jingled.

"I drink," he said, "to the buried that repose around us."

"And I to your long life."

L

He again took my arm, and we proceeded.

"These vaults," he said, "are extensive."

"The Montresors," I replied, "were a great and numerous family."

"I forget your arms."

"A huge human foot d'or, in a field azure; the foot crushes a serpent rampant whose fangs are imbedded in the heel."

"And the motto?"

"Nemo me impune lacessit." [23]

"Good!" he said.

The wine sparkled in his eyes and the bells jingled. My own fancy grew warm with the Médoc. We had passed through walls of piled bones, with casks and puncheons intermingling, into the inmost recesses of the catacombs. I paused again, and this time I made bold to seize Fortunato by an arm above the elbow.

"The niter!" I said, "see, it increases. It hangs like moss upon the vaults. We are below the river's bed. The drops of moisture trickle among the bones. Come, we will go back ere it is too late. Your cough — "

"It is nothing," he said, "let us go on. But first, another draught of the Médoc."

I broke and reached him a flagon of De Grâve. He emptied it at a breath. His eyes

[23] *Nemo me impune lacessit* — No one provokes me with impunity. (Compare this with the motto on the Gadsden flag of 1775, which also shows a snake: "Don't tread on me." This device was apparently very popular in Revolutionary days. The snake was a rattler with 13 rattles — one for each colony.)

flashed with a fierce light. He laughed and threw the bottle upward with a gesticulation I did not understand.

I looked at him in surprise. He repeated the movement — a grotesque one.

"You do not comprehend?" he said.

"Not I," I replied.

"Then you are not of the brotherhood."

"How?"

"You are not of the masons."

"Yes, yes," I said, "yes, yes."

"You? Impossible! A mason?"

"A mason," I replied.

"A sign," he said.

"It is this," I answered, producing a trowel from beneath the folds of my *roquelaire*.

"You jest," he exclaimed, recoiling a few paces. "But let us proceed to the Amontillado."

"Be it so," I said, replacing the tool beneath the cloak, and again offering him my arm. He leaned upon it heavily. We continued our route in search of the Amontillado. We passed through a range of low arches, descended, passed on, and descending again, arrived at a deep crypt, in which the foulness of the air caused our flambeaux rather to glow than flame.

At the most remote end of the crypt there appeared another less spacious. Its walls had been lined with human remains, piled to the vault overhead, in the fashion of the great catacombs of Paris. Three sides of this interior crypt were still ornamented in this manner. From the fourth the bones had been thrown down, and lay promiscuously upon the earth, forming at one point a mound of some size. Within the wall thus exposed by the displacing of the bones, we perceived a still interior recess, in depth about four feet, in width three, in height six or seven. It seemed to have been constructed for no especial use within itself, but formed merely the interval between two of the colossal supports of the roof of the catacombs, and was backed by one of their circumscribing walls of solid granite.

It was in vain that Fortunato, uplifting his dull torch, endeavored to pry into the depth of the recess. Its termination the feeble light did not enable us to see.

"Proceed," I said, "herein is the Amontillado. As for Luchesi — "

"He is an ignoramus," interrupted my friend, as he stepped unsteadily forward, while I followed, immediately at his heels. In an instant he had reached the extremity of the niche and, finding his progress arrested by the rock, stood stupidly bewildered. A moment more and I had fettered him to the granite. In its surface were two iron staples, distant from each other about two feet, horizontally. From one of these depended a short chain, from the other a padlock. Throwing the links about his waist, it was but the work of a few seconds to secure it. He was too much astounded to resist. Withdrawing the key, I stepped back from the recess.

"Pass your hand," I said, "over the wall; you

cannot help feeling the niter. Indeed it is *very* damp. Once more let me *implore* you to return. No? Then I must positively leave you. But I must first render you all the little attentions in my power."

"The Amontillado!" ejaculated my friend, not yet recovered from his astonishment.

"True," I replied, "the Amontillado."

As I said these words I busied myself among the pile of bones of which I have before spoken. Throwing them aside, I soon uncovered a quantity of building stone and mortar. With these materials and with the aid of my trowel, I began vigorously to wall up the entrance of the niche.

I had scarcely laid the first tier of the masonry when I discovered that the intoxication of Fortunato had in a great measure worn off. The earliest indication I had of this was a low moaning cry from the depth of the recess. It was *not* the cry of a drunken man. There was then a long and obstinate silence. I laid the second tier, and the third, and the fourth; and then I heard the furious vibrations of the chain. The noise lasted for several minutes, during which, that I might hearken to it with the more satisfaction, I ceased my labors and sat down upon the bones. When at last the clanking subsided, I resumed the trowel, and finished without interruption the fifth, the sixth, and the seventh tier. The wall was now nearly upon a level with my breast. I again paused and, holding the flambeaux over the mason work, threw a few feeble rays upon the figure within.

A succession of loud and shrill screams, bursting suddenly from the throat of the chained form, seemed to thrust me violently back. For a brief moment I hesitated — I trembled. Unsheathing my rapier, I began to grope with it about the recess; but the thought of an instant reassured me. I placed my hand upon the solid fabric of the catacombs, and felt satisfied. I reapproached the wall. I replied to the yells of him who clamored. I reechoed — I aided — surpassed them in volume and in strength. I did this, and the clamorer grew still.

It was now midnight, and my task was drawing to a close. I had completed the eighth, the ninth, and the tenth tier. I had finished a portion of the last and the eleventh; there remained but a single stone to be fitted and plastered in. I struggled with its weight; I placed it partially in its destined position. But now there came out the niche a low laugh that erected the hairs upon my head. It was succeeded by a sad voice, which I had difficulty in recognizing as that of the noble Fortunato. The voice said —

"Ha ha! ha! — he! he! — a very good joke indeed — an excellent jest. We will have many a rich laugh about it at the palazzo — he! he! he! — over our wine — he! he! he!"

"The Amontillado!" I said.

"He! he! he! — he! he! he! — yes, the Amontillado. But is it not getting late? Will not they be awaiting us at the palazzo, the Lady Fortunato and the rest? Let us be gone."

"Yes," I said, "let us be gone."

"For the love of God, Montresor!"

"Yes," I said, "for the love of God!"

But to these words I hearkened in vain for a reply. I grew impatient. I called aloud:

"Fortunato!"

No answer. I called again:

"Fortunato!"

No answer still. I thrust a torch through the remaining aperture and let it fall within. There came forth in return only a jingling of the bells. My heart grew sick — on account of the dampness of the catacombs. I hastened to make an end of my labor. I forced the last stone into its position; I plastered it up. Against the new masonry I reerected the old rampart of bones. For the half of a century no mortal has disturbed them. *In pace requiescat!*

THE FALL OF THE HOUSE
OF USHER

Son cœur est un luth suspendu;
Sitôt qu-on le touche il résonne.[24]
— *De Béranger*

DURING the whole of a dull, dark, and sound-
less day in the autumn of the year, when
the clouds hung oppressively low in the heavens,
I had been passing alone, on horseback,
through a singularly dreary tract of country,
and at length found myself, as the shades of the
evening drew on, within view of the melancholy
House of Usher. I know not how it was — but,
with the first glimpse of the building, a sense of
insufferable gloom pervaded my spirit. I say insufferable; for the feeling was unrelieved by any
of that half-pleasurable, because poetic, sentiment with which the mind usually receives even
the sternest natural images of the desolate or
terrible. I looked upon the scene before me —
upon the mere house, and the simple landscape

24 *Son cœur . . . résonne* — His heart is a suspended lute,
as soon as someone touches it, it resounds.

features of the domain — upon the bleak walls
— upon the vacant eyelike windows — upon a
few rank sedges — and upon a few white trunks
of decayed trees — with an utter depression of
soul which I can compare to no earthly sensation more properly than to the afterdream of
the reveler upon opium — the bitter lapse into
everyday life — the hideous dropping off of the
veil. There was an iciness, a sinking, a sickening of the heart — an unredeemed dreariness of
thought which no goading of the imagination
could torture into aught of the sublime. What
was it — I paused to think — what was it that so
unnerved me in the contemplation of the House
of Usher? It was a mystery all insoluble; nor
could I grapple with the shadowy fancies that
crowded upon me as I pondered. I was forced
to fall back upon the unsatisfactory conclusion
that while, beyond doubt, there *are* combina-
tions of very simple natural objects which have
the power of thus affecting us, still the analysis
of this power lies among considerations beyond
our depth. It was possible, I reflected, that a
mere different arrangement of the particulars of
the scene, of the details of the picture, would be
sufficient to modify, or perhaps to annihilate,
its capacity for sorrowful impression; and, act-
ing upon this idea, I reined my horse to the precipitous brink of a black and lurid tarn that lay
in unruffled lustre by the dwelling, and gazed
down — but with a shudder even more thrilling
than before — upon the remodeled and inverted

images of the gray sedge, and the ghastly tree stems, and the vacant and eyelike windows.

Nevertheless, in this mansion of gloom I now proposed to myself a sojourn of some weeks. Its proprietor, Roderick Usher, had been one of my boon companions in boyhood; but many years had elapsed since our last meeting. A letter, however, had lately reached me in a distant part of the country — a letter from him — which, in its wildly importunate nature, had admitted of no other than a personal reply. The ms. gave evidence of nervous agitation. The writer spoke of acute bodily illness — of a mental disorder which oppressed him — and of an earnest desire to see me, as his best and indeed his only personal friend, with a view of attempting, by the cheerfulness of my society, some alleviation of his malady. It was the manner in which all this, and much more, was said — it was the apparent *heart* that went with his request — which allowed me no room for hesitation; and I accordingly obeyed forthwith what I still considered a very singular summons.

Although, as boys, we had been even intimate associates, yet I really knew little of my friend. His reserve had been always excessive and habitual. I was aware, however, that his very ancient family had been noted, time out of mind, for a peculiar sensibility of temperament, displaying itself, through long ages, in many works of exalted art, and manifested, of late, in repeated deeds of munificent yet unobtrusive charity, as well as in a passionate devotion to the intricacies, perhaps even more than to the orthodox and easily recognizable beauties, of musical science. I had learned, too, the very remarkable fact, that the stem of the Usher race, all time-honored as it was, had put forth, at no period, any enduring branch; in other words, that the entire family lay in the direct line of descent, and had always, with very trifling and very temporary variation, so lain. It was this deficiency, I considered, while running over in thought the perfect keeping of the character of the premises with the accredited character of the people, and while speculating upon the possible influence which the one, in the long lapse of centuries, might have exercised upon the other — it was this deficiency, perhaps, of collateral issue, and the consequent undeviating transmission, from sire to son, of the patrimony with the name, which had, at length, so identified the two as to merge the original title of the estate in the quaint and equivocal appellation of the "House of Usher" — an appellation which seemed to include, in the minds of the peasantry who used it, both the family and the family mansion.

I have said that the sole effect of my somewhat childish experiment — that of looking down within the tarn — had been to deepen the first singular impression. There can be no doubt that the consciousness of the rapid increase of my superstition — for why should I not so term it? — served mainly to accelerate the increase itself. Such, I have long known, is the paradoxical law of all sentiments having terror as a basis. And it might have been for this reason only, that, when I again uplifted my eyes to the house itself, from its image in the pool, there grew in my mind a strange fancy — a fancy so ridiculous, indeed, that I but mention it to show the vivid force of the sensations which oppressed me. I had so worked upon my imagination as really to believe that about the whole mansion and domain there hung an atmosphere peculiar to themselves and their immediate vicinity — an atmosphere which had no affinity with the air of heaven, but which had reeked up from the decayed trees, and the gray wall, and the silent tarn — a pestilent and mystic vapor, dull, sluggish, faintly discernible, and leaden-hued.

Shaking off from my spirit what *must* have been a dream, I scanned more narrowly the real aspect of the building. Its principal feature seemed to be that of an excessive antiquity. The discoloration of ages had been great. Minute fungi overspread the whole exterior, hanging in a fine tangled webwork from the eaves. Yet all this was apart from an extraordinary dilapidation. No portion of the masonry had fallen, and there appeared to be a wild inconsistency between its still perfect adaptation of parts and the crumbling condition of the individual stones. In this there was much that reminded me of the specious totality of old woodwork

which has rotted for long years in some neglected vault, with no disturbance from the
breath of the external air. Beyond this indication of extensive decay, however, the fabric gave
little token of instability. Perhaps the eye of a
scrutinizing observer might have discovered a
barely perceptible fissure, which, extending
from the roof of the building in front, made its
way down the wall in a zigzag direction, until it
became lost in the sullen waters of the tarn.

Noticing these things, I rode over a short
causeway to the house. A servant in waiting took
my horse, and I entered the Gothic archway of
the hall. A valet, of stealthy step, thence con-
ducted me, in silence, through many dark and
intricate passages in my progress to the studio
of his master. Much that I encountered on the
way contributed, I know not how, to heighten
the vague sentiments of which I have already
spoken. While the objects around me — while
the carvings of the ceilings, the somber tapestries of the walls, the ebony blackness of the
floors, and the phantasmagoric armorial tro-
phies which rattled as I strode, were but matters to which, or to such as which, I had been
accustomed from my infancy — while I hesitated
not to acknowledge how familiar was all this —
I still wondered to find how unfamiliar were
the fancies which ordinary images were stirring
up. On one of the staircases, I met the physician
of the family. His countenance, I thought, wore
a mingled expression of low cunning and per-

plexity. He accosted me with trepidation and passed on. The valet now threw open a door and ushered me into the presence of his master.

The room in which I found myself was very large and lofty. The windows were long, narrow, and pointed, and at so vast a distance from the black oaken floor as to be altogether inaccessible from within. Feeble gleams of encrimsoned light made their way through the trellised panes, and served to render sufficiently distinct the more prominent objects around; the eye, however, struggled in vain to reach the remoter angles of the chamber, or the recesses of the vaulted and fretted ceiling. Dark draperies hung upon the walls. The general furniture was profuse, comfortless, antique, and tattered. Many books and musical instruments lay scattered about, but failed to give any vitality to the scene. I felt that I breathed an atmosphere of sorrow. An air of stern, deep, and irredeemable gloom hung over and pervaded all.

Upon my entrance, Usher arose from a sofa on which he had been lying at full length, and greeted me with a vivacious warmth which had much in it, I at first thought, of an overdone cordiality — of the constrained effort of the *ennuyé* [25] man of the world. A glance, however, at his countenance convinced me of his perfect sincerity. We sat down; and for some moments, while he spoke not, I gazed upon him with a feeling half of pity, half of awe. Surely, man

25 *ennuyé* — bored.

had never before so terribly altered, in so brief a period, as had Roderick Usher! It was with difficulty that I could bring myself to admit the identity of the wan being before me with the companion of my early boyhood. Yet the character of his face had been at all times remarkable. A cadaverousness of complexion; an eye large, liquid, and luminous beyond comparison; lips somewhat thin and very pallid, but of a surpassingly beautiful curve; a nose of a delicate Hebrew model, but with a breadth of nostril unusual in similar formations; a finely molded chin, speaking, in its want of prominence, of a want of moral energy; hair of a more than web-like softness and tenuity — these features, with an inordinate expansion above the regions of the temple, made up altogether a countenance not easily to be forgotten. And now in the mere exaggeration of the prevailing character of these features, and of the expression they were wont to convey, lay so much of change that I doubted to whom I spoke. The now ghastly pallor of the skin, and the now miraculous lustre of the eye, above all things startled and even awed me. The silken hair, too, had been suffered to grow all unheeded and, as, in its wild gossamer texture, it floated rather than fell about the face, I could not, even with effort, connect its arabesque expression with any idea of simple humanity.

In the manner of my friend I was at once struck with an incoherence — an inconsistency; and I soon found this to arise from a series of feeble and futile struggles to overcome an habitual trepidancy — an excessive nervous agitation. For something of this nature I had indeed been prepared, no less by his letter than by reminiscences of certain boyish traits, and by conclusions deduced from his peculiar physical confirmation and temperament. His action was alternately vivacious and sullen. His voice varied rapidly from a tremulous indecision (when the animal spirits seemed utterly in abeyance) to that species of energetic concision — that abrupt, weighty, unhurried, and hollow-sounding enunciation — that leaden, self-balanced, and perfectly modulated guttural utterance, which may be observed in the lost drunkard, or the irreclaimable eater of opium, during the periods of his most intense excitement.

It was thus that he spoke of the object of my visit, of his earnest desire to see me, and of the solace he expected me to afford him. He entered, at some length, into what he conceived to be the nature of his malady. It was, he said, a constitutional and a family evil, and one for which he despaired to find a remedy — a mere nervous affection, he immediately added, which would undoubtedly soon pass off. It displayed itself in a host of unnatural sensations. Some of these, as he detailed them, interested and bewildered me; although, perhaps, the terms and the general manner of their narration had their weight. He suffered much from a morbid acuteness of the senses; the most insipid food was alone endurable; he could wear only garments of certain texture; the odors of all flowers were oppressive; his eyes were tortured by even a faint light; and there were but peculiar sounds, and these from stringed instruments, which did not inspire him with horror.

To an anomalous species of terror I found him a bounden slave. "I shall perish," said he, "*I must perish* in this deplorable folly. Thus, thus and not otherwise, shall I be lost. I dread the events of the future, not in themselves, but in their results. I shudder at the thought of any, even the most trivial, incident which may operate upon this intolerable agitation of soul. I have, indeed, no abhorrence of danger, except in its absolute effect — in terror. In this unnerved, in this pitiable, condition I feel that the period will sooner or later arrive when I must abandon life and reason together, in some struggle with the grim phantasm, FEAR."

I learned, moreover, at intervals, and through broken and equivocal hints, another singular feature of his mental condition. He was enchained by certain superstitious impressions in regard to the dwelling which he tenanted, and from whence, for many years, he had never ventured forth — in regard to an influence whose supposititous force was conveyed in terms too shadowy here to be restated — an influence which some peculiarities in the mere form and substance of his family mansion had, by dint of long sufferance, he said, obtained over his spirit — an effect which the *physique* of the gray walls and turrets, and of the dim tarn into which they all looked down, had, at length, brought about upon the *morale* of his existence.

He admitted, however, although with hesitation, that much of the peculiar gloom which thus afflicted him could be traced to a more natural and far more palpable origin — to the severe and long-continued illness, indeed to the evidently approaching dissolution — of a tenderly beloved sister, his sole companion for long years, his last and only relative on earth. "Her decease," he said, with a bitterness which I can never forget, "would leave me [him, the hopeless and the frail] the last of the ancient race of the Ushers." While he spoke the Lady Madeline (for so was she called) passed through a remote portion of the apartment, and, without having noticed my presence, disappeared. I regarded her with an utter astonishment not unmingled with dread; and yet I found it impossible to account for such feelings. A sensation of stupor oppressed me as my eyes followed her retreating steps. When a door, at length, closed upon her, my glance sought instinctively and eagerly the countenance of the brother; but he had buried his face in his hands, and I could only perceive that a far more than ordinary wanness had overspread the emaciated fingers through which trickled many passionate tears.

The disease of the Lady Madeline had long

baffled the skill of her physicians. A settled apathy, a gradual wasting away of the person, and frequent although transient affections of a partially cataleptical character were the unusual diagnosis. Hitherto she had steadily borne up against the pressure of her malady, and had not betaken herself finally to bed; but on the closing in of the evening of my arrival at the house, she succumbed (as her brother told me at night with inexpressible agitation) to the prostrating power of the destroyer; and I learned that the glimpse I had obtained of her person would thus probably be the last I should obtain — that the lady, at least while living, would be seen by me no more.

For several days ensuing, her name was unmentioned by either Usher or myself; and during this period I was busied in earnest endeavors to alleviate the melancholy of my friend. We painted and read together, or I listened, as if in a dream, to the wild improvisations of his speaking guitar. And thus, as a closer and still closer intimacy admitted me more unreservedly into the recesses of his spirit, the more bitterly did I perceive the futility of all attempt at cheering a mind from which darkness, as if an inherent positive quality, poured forth upon all objects of the moral and physical universe in one unceasing radiation of gloom.

I shall ever bear about me a memory of the many solemn hours I thus spent alone with the master of the House of Usher. Yet I should fail in any attempt to convey an idea of the exact character of the studies, or of the occupations, in which he involved me, or led me the way. An excited and highly distempered ideality threw a sulfureous lustre over all. His long improvised dirges will ring forever in my ears. Among other things, I hold painfully in mind a certain singular perversion and amplification of the wild air of the last waltz of Von Weber. From the paintings over which his elaborate fancy brooded, and which grew, touch by touch, into vaguenesses at which I shuddered the more thrillingly, because I shuddered knowing not why — from these paintings (vivid as their images now are before me) I would in vain endeavor to educe more than a small portion which should lie within the compass of merely written words. By the utter simplicity, by the nakedness of his designs, he arrested and overawed attention. If ever mortal painted an idea, that mortal was Roderick Usher. For me at least, in the circumstances then surrounding me, there arose out of the pure abstractions which the hypochondriac contrived to throw upon his canvas, an intensity of intolerable awe, no shadow of which felt I ever yet in the contemplation of the certainly glowing yet too concrete reveries of Fuseli.

One of the phantasmagoric conceptions of my friend, partaking not so rigidly of the spirit of abstraction, may be shadowed forth, although feebly, in words. A small picture presented the interior of an immensely long and rectangular vault or tunnel, with low walls, smooth, white, and without interruption or device. Certain accessory points of the design served well to convey the idea that this excavation lay at an exceeding depth below the surface of the earth. No outlet was observed in any portion of its vast extent, and no torch or other artificial source of light was discernible; yet a flood of intense rays rolled throughout, and bathed the whole in a ghastly and inappropriate splendor.

I have just spoken of the morbid condition of the auditory nerve which rendered all music intolerable to the sufferer, with the exception of certain effects of stringed instruments. It was, perhaps, the narrow limits to which he thus confined himself upon the guitar which gave birth, in great measure, to the fantastic character of his performances. But the fervid facility of his impromptus could not be so accounted for. They must have been, and were, in the notes, as well as in the words of his wild fantasias (for he not unfrequently accompanied himself with rhymed verbal improvisations), the result of that intense mental collectedness and concentration to which I have previously alluded as observable only in particular moments of the highest artificial excitement. The words of one of these rhapsodies I have easily remembered. I was, perhaps, the more forcibly impressed with it as he gave it, because, in the under or mystic current of its meaning, I fancied that I perceived, and for the first time, a full consciousness on the part of Usher of the tottering of his lofty reason upon her throne. The verses, which were entitled "The Haunted Palace," ran very nearly, if not accurately, thus:

In the greenest of our valleys,
  By good angels tenanted,
Once a fair and stately palace —
  Radiant palace — reared its head.
In the monarch Thought's dominion —
  It stood there!
Never seraph spread a pinion
  Over fabric half so fair.

Banners yellow, glorious, golden,
  On its roof did float and flow
(This — all this — was in the olden
  Time long ago);
And every gentle air that dallied,
  In that sweet day,
A winged odor went away.

Wanderers in that happy valley
  Through two luminous windows saw
Spirits playing musically
  To a lute's well-tuned law;
Round about a throne, where sitting
  (Porphyrogene!)
In state his glory well befitting,
  The ruler of the realm was seen.

And all with pearl and ruby glowing
  Was the fair palace door,
Through which came flowing, flowing, flowing
  And sparkling evermore,
A troop of Echoes whose sweet duty
  Was but to sing,
In voices of surpassing beauty,
  The wit and wisdom of their king.

But evil things, in robes of sorrow,
  Assailed the monarch's high estate;
(Ah, let us mourn, for never morrow
  Shall dawn upon him, desolate!)

And, round about his home, the glory
   That blushed and bloomed
Is but a dim-remembered story
   Of the old time entombed.

And travelers now within that valley,
   Through the red-litten windows see
Vast forms that move fantastically
   To a discordant melody;
While, like a rapid ghastly river,
   Through the pale door;
A hideous throng rush out forever,
   And laugh — but smile no more.

I well remember that suggestions arising from
this ballad led us into a train of thought where-
in there became manifest an opinion of Usher's
which I mention not so much on account of its
novelty (for other men have thought thus), as
on account of the pertinacity with which he
maintained it. This opinion, in its general form,
was that of the sentience of all vegetable things.
But, in his disordered fancy, the idea had assumed a more daring character, and trespassed,
under certain conditions, upon the kingdom of
inorganization. I lack words to express the full
extent, or the earnest *abandon* of his persua-
sion. The belief, however, was connected (as I
have previously hinted) with the gray stones of
the home of his forefathers. The conditions of
the sentience had been here, he imagined, ful-
filled in the method of, collocation [26] of, these
stones — in the order of their arrangement, as
well as in that of the many fungi which overspread them, and of the decayed trees which

[26] collocation — arranging together, positioning.

stood around — above all, in the long undisturbed endurance of this arrangement, and in
its reduplication in the still waters of the tarn.
Its evidence — the evidence of the sentience —
was to be seen, he said (and I here started as he
spoke), in the gradual yet certain condensation
of an atmosphere of their own about the waters
and the walls. The result was discoverable, he
added, in that silent yet importunate and terrible influence which for centuries had molded
the destinies of his family, and which made
him what I now saw him — what he was. Such
opinions need no comment, and I will make
none.

Our books — the books which, for years, had
formed no small portion of the mental existence
of the invalid — were, as might be supposed, in
strict keeping with this character of phantasm.
We pored together over such works as the *Ver-
vert et Chartreuse* of Gresset; the *Belphegor* of
Machiavelli; the *Heaven and Hell* of Sweden-
borg; the *Subterranean Voyage of Nicholas
Klimm* of Holberg; the *Chiromancy* of Robert
Flud, of Jean d'Indaginé, and of De la Cham-
bre; the *Journey into the Blue Distance* of
Tieck; and the *City of the Sun* of Campanella.
One favorite volume was a small octavo edition
of the *Directorium Inquisitorium*, by the
Dominican Eymeric de Gironne; and there
were passages in Pomponius Mela, about the
old African satyrs and egipans, over which
Usher would sit dreaming for hours. His chief

delight, however, was found in the perusal of an exceedingly rare and curious book in quarto Gothic — the manual of a forgotten church — *the Vigiliæ Mortuorum secundum Chorum Ecclesiæ Maguntinæ.*

I could not help thinking of the wild ritual of this work, and of its probable influence upon the hypochondriac, when, one evening, having informed me abruptly that the Lady Madeline was no more, he stated his intention of preserving her corpse for a fortnight (previously to its final interment), in one of the numerous vaults within the main walls of the building. The worldly reason, however, assigned for this singular proceeding, was one which I did not feel at liberty to dispute. The brother had been led to his resolution (so he told me) by consideration of the unusual character of the malady of the deceased, of certain obtrusive and eager inquiries on the part of her medical men, and of the remote and exposed situation of the burial ground of the family. I will not deny that when I called to mind the sinister countenance of the person whom I met upon the staircase, on the day of my arrival at the house, I had no desire to oppose what I regarded as at best but a harmless, and by no means an unnatural, precaution.

At the request of Usher, I personally aided him in the arrangements for the temporary entombment. The body having been encoffined, we two alone bore it to its rest. The vault in which we placed it (and which had been so long unopened that our torches, half smothered in its oppressive atmosphere, gave us little opportunity for investigation) was small, damp, and entirely without means of admission for light; lying, at great depth, immediately beneath that portion of the building in which was my own sleeping apartment. It had been used, apparently, in remote feudal times, for the worst purposes of a dungeon keep, and, in later days, as a place of deposit for powder, or some other highly combustible substance, as a portion of its floor and the whole interior of a long archway through which we reached it were carefully sheathed with copper. The door, of massive iron, had been, also, similarly protected. Its immense weight caused an unusually sharp, grating sound, as it moved upon its hinges.

Having deposited our mournful burden upon tressels within this region of horror, we partially turned aside the yet unscrewed lid of the coffin, and looked upon the face of the tenant. A striking similitude between the brother and sister now first arrested my attention; and Usher, divining, perhaps, my thoughts, murmured out some few words from which I learned that the deceased and himself had been twins, and that sympathies of a scarcely intelligible nature had always existed between them. Our glances, however, rested not long upon the dead — for we could not regard her unawed. The disease which had thus entombed the lady in the maturity of youth, had left, as usual in all maladies of a strictly cataleptical character, the mockery of a faint blush upon the bosom and the face, and that suspiciously lingering smile upon the lip which is so terrible in death. We replaced and screwed down the lid, and, having secured the door of iron, made our way, with toil, into the scarcely less gloomy apartments of the upper portion of the house.

And now, some days of bitter grief having elapsed, an observable change came over the features of the mental disorder of my friend. His ordinary manner had vanished. His ordinary occupations were neglected or forgotten. He roamed from chamber to chamber with hurried, unequal, and objectless step. The pallor of his countenance had assumed, if possible, a more ghastly hue — but the luminousness of his eye had utterly gone out. The once occasional huskiness of his tone was heard no more; and a tremulous quaver, as if of extreme terror, habitually characterized his utterance. There were times, indeed, when I thought his unceasingly agitated mind was laboring with some oppressive secret, to divulge which he struggled for the necessary courage. At times, again, I was obliged to resolve all into the mere inexplicable vagaries of madness, for I beheld him gazing upon vacancy for long hours, in an attitude of the profoundest attention, as if listening to some imaginary sound. It was no wonder that his condition terrified — that it infected me. I felt creeping upon me, by slow yet certain degrees, the wild influences of his own fantastic yet impressive superstitions.

It was, especially, upon retiring to bed late in the night of the seventh or eighth day after the placing of the Lady Madeline within the dungeon, that I experienced the full power of such feelings. Sleep came not near my couch — while the hours waned and waned away. I struggled to reason off the nervousness which had dominion over me. I endeavored to believe that much, if not all of what I felt, was due to the bewildering influence of the gloomy furniture of the room — of the dark and tattered draperies, which, tortured into motion by the breath of a rising tempest, swayed fitfully to and fro upon the walls, and rustled uneasily about the decorations of the bed. But my efforts were fruitless. An irrepressible tremor gradually pervaded my frame; and, at length, there sat upon my very heart an incubus of utterly causeless alarm. Shaking this off with a gasp and a struggle, I uplifted myself upon the pillows, and, peering earnestly within the intense darkness of the chamber, hearkened — I know not why, except that an instinctive spirit prompted me — to certain low and indefinite sounds which came, through the pauses of the storm, at long intervals, I knew not whence. Overpowered by an intense sentiment of horror, unaccountable yet unendurable, I threw on my clothes with haste (for I felt that I should sleep no more during the night), and endeavored to arouse myself from the pitiable condition into which I had fallen, by pacing rapidly to and fro through the apartment.

I had taken but few turns in this manner when a light step on an adjoining staircase arrested my attention. I presently recognized it as that of Usher. In an instant afterward he rapped, with a gentle touch, at my door, and entered, bearing a lamp. His countenance was, as usual, cadaverously wan — but, moreover, there was a species of mad hilarity in his eyes — an evidently restrained hysteria in his whole demeanor. His air appalled me — but anything was preferable to the solitude which I had so long endured, and I even welcomed his presence as a relief.

"And you have not seen it?" he said abruptly, after having stared about him for some moments in silence. "You have not then seen it? — but, stay! you shall." Thus speaking, and having carefully shaded his lamp, he hurried to one of the casements, and threw it freely open to the storm.

The impetuous fury of the entering gust nearly lifted us from our feet. It was, indeed, a tempestuous yet sternly beautiful night, and one wildly singular in its terror and its beauty. A whirlwind had apparently collected its force in our vicinity for there were frequent and violent alterations in the direction of the wind; and the exceeding density of the clouds (which hung so low as to press upon the turrets of the house) did not prevent our perceiving the life-like velocity with which they flew careering from all points against each other, without passing away into the distance. I say that even their exceeding density did not prevent our perceiving this — yet we had no glimpse of the moon or stars, nor was there any flashing forth of the lightning. But the undersurfaces of the huge masses of agitated vapor, as well as all terrestrial objects immediately around us, were glowing in the unnatural light of a faintly luminous and distinctly visible gaseous exhalation which hung about and enshrouded the mansion.

"You must not — you shall not behold this!" said I, shuddering, to Usher, as I led him, with a gentle violence, from the window to a seat. "These appearances, which bewilder you, are merely electrical phenomena, not uncommon — or it may be that they have their ghastly origin in the rank miasma of the tarn. Let us close this casement; the air is chilling and dangerous to your frame. Here is one of your favorite romances. I will read, and you shall listen — and so we will pass away this terrible night together."

The antique volume which I had taken up was the *Mad Trist* of Sir Launcelot Canning; but I had called it a favorite of Usher's more in sad jest than in earnest; for, in truth, there is little in its uncouth and unimaginative prolixity which could have had interest for the lofty and spiritual ideality of my friend. It was, however, the only book immediately at hand; and I indulged a vague hope that the excitement which now agitated the hypochondriac might find relief (for the history of mental disorder is full of similar anomalies) even in the extremeness of the folly which I should read. Could I have judged, indeed, by the wild overstrained air of vivacity with which he hearkened, or apparently hearkened, to the words of the tale, I might well have congratulated myself upon the success of my design.

I had arrived at that well-known portion of the story where Ethelred, the hero of the *Trist*, having sought in vain for peaceable admission into the dwelling of the hermit, proceeds to make good an entrance by force. Here, it will be remembered, the words of the narrative run thus:

"And Ethelred, who was by nature of a doughty heart, and who was now mighty withal, on account of the powerfulness of the wine which he had drunken, waited no longer to hold parley with the hermit, who, in sooth, was of an obstinate and maliceful turn, but, feeling the rain upon his shoulders, and fearing the rising of the tempest, uplifted his mace outright, and, with blows, made quickly room in the plankings of the door for his gauntleted hand; and now pulling therewith sturdily, he so cracked, and ripped, and tore all asunder, that the noise of the dry and hollow-sounding wood alarumed and reverberated throughout the forest."

At the termination of this sentence I started and, for a moment, paused; for it appeared to me (although I at once concluded that my excited fancy had deceived me) — it appeared to me that, from some very remote portion of the mansion, there came, indistinctly to my ears, what might have been, in its exact similarity of character, the echo (but a stifled and dull one certainly) of the very cracking and ripping sound which Sir Launcelot had so particularly described. It was, beyond doubt, the coincidence alone which had arrested my attention; for, amid the rattling of the sashes of the casements, and the ordinary commingled noises of the still increasing storm, the sound in itself had nothing, surely, which should have interested or disturbed me. I continued the story:

"But the good champion Ethelred, now entering within the door, was sore enraged and amazed to perceive no signal of the maliceful hermit; but, in the stead thereof, a dragon of a scaly and prodigious demeanor, and of a fiery tongue, which sate in guard before a palace of gold, with a floor of silver; and upon the wall there hung a shield of shining brass with this legend enwritten:
Who entereth herein, a conqueror hath bin;
Who slayeth the dragon, the shield he shall win.
And Ethelred uplifted his mace, and struck upon the head of the dragon, which fell before

him, and gave up his pasty breath, with a shriek so horrid and harsh, and withal so piercing, that Ethelred had fain to close his ears with his hands against the dreadful noise of it, the like whereof was never before heard."

Here again I paused abruptly, and now with a feeling of wild amazement — for there could be no doubt whatever that, in this instance, I did actually hear (although from what direction it proceeded I found it impossible to say) a low and apparently distant, but harsh, protracted, and most unusual screaming or grating sound — the exact counterpart of what my fancy had already conjured up for the dragon's unnatural shriek as described by the romancer.

Oppressed, as I certainly was, upon the occurrence of this second and most extraordinary coincidence, by a thousand conflicting sensations, in which wonder and extreme terror were predominant, I still retained sufficient presence of mind to avoid exciting, by any observation, the sensitive nervousness of my companion. I was by no means certain that he had noticed the sounds in question; although, assuredly, a strange alteration had, during the last few minutes, taken place in his demeanor. From a position fronting my own, he had gradually brought round his chair, so as to sit with his face to the door of the chamber; and thus I could but partially perceive his features, although I saw that his lips trembled as if he were murmuring inaudibly. His head had dropped upon his breast — yet I knew that he was not asleep, from the wide and rigid opening of the eye as I caught a glance of it in profile. The motion of his body, too, was at variance with this idea — for he rocked from side to side with a gentle yet constant and uniform sway. Having rapidly taken notice of all this, I resumed the narrative of Sir Launcelot, which thus proceeded:

"And now, the champion, having escaped from the terrible fury of the dragon, bethinking himself of the brazen shield, and of the breaking up of the enchantment which was upon it, removed the carcass from out of the way before him, and approached valorously over the silver pavement of the castle to where the shield was upon the wall; which in sooth tarried not for his full coming, but fell down at his feet upon the silver floor, with a mighty great and terrible ringing sound."

No sooner had these syllables passed my lips, than — as if a shield of brass had indeed, at the moment, fallen heavily upon a floor of silver — I became aware of a distinct, hollow, metallic, and clangorous, yet apparently muffled, reverberation. Completely unnerved, I leaped to my feet; but the measured rocking movement of Usher was undisturbed. I rushed to the chair in which he sat. His eyes were bent fixedly before him, and throughout his whole countenance there reigned a stony rigidity. But, as I placed my hand upon his shoulder, there came a strong shudder over his whole person; a sickly smile quivered about his lips; and I saw that he spoke in a low, hurried, and gibbering murmur, as if unconscious of my presence. Bending closely over him, I at length drank in the hideous import of his words.

"Now hear it? — yes, I hear it, and *have* heard it. Long — long — long — many minutes, many hours, many days have I heard it — yet I dared not — oh, pity me, miserable wretch that I am! — I dared not — I *dared* not speak! *We have put her living in the tomb!* Said I not that my senses were acute? I *now* tell you that I heard her first feeble movements in the hollow coffin. I heard them — many, many days ago — yet I dared not — *I dared not speak!* And now — tonight — Ethelred — ha! ha! — the breaking of the hermit's door, and the death cry of the dragon, and the clangor of the shield — say, rather, the rending of her coffin, and the grating of the iron hinges of her prison, and her struggles within the coppered archway of the vault! Oh! whither shall I fly? Will she not be here anon? Is she not hurrying to upbraid me for my haste? Have I not heard her footstep on the stair? Do I distinguish that heavy and horrible beating of her heart? Madman!" — here he sprang furiously to his feet, and shieked out his syllables, as if in the effort he were giving up his soul — *"Madman! I tell you that she now stands without the door!"*

As if in the superhuman energy of his utterance there had been found the potency of a spell, the huge antique panels to which the speaker pointed threw slowly back, upon the instant, their ponderous and ebony jaws. It was the work of the rushing gust — but then without those doors there *did* stand the lofty and enshrouded figure of the Lady Madeline of Usher. There was blood upon her white robes, and the evidence of some bitter struggle upon every portion of her emaciated frame. For a moment she remained trembling and reeling to and fro upon the threshold — then, with a low moaning cry, fell heavily inward upon the person of her brother, and in her violent and now final death agonies, bore him to the floor a corpse, and a victim to the terrors he had anticipated.

From that chamber, and from that mansion, I fled aghast. The storm was still abroad in all its wrath as I found myself crossing the old causeway. Suddenly there shot along the path a wild light, and I turned to see whence a gleam so unusual could have issued; for the vast house and its shadows were alone behind me. The radiance was that of the full, setting, and blood-red moon, which now shone vividly through that once barely discernible fissure, of which I have before spoken as extending from the roof of the building, in a zigzag direction, to the base. While I gazed, this fissure rapidly widened — there came a fierce breath of the whirlwind — the entire orb of the satellite burst at once upon my sight — my brain reeled as I saw the mighty walls rushing asunder — there was a long tumultuous shouting sound like the voice of a thousand waters — and the deep and dank tarn at my feet closed sullenly and silently over the fragments of the *House of Usher.*

THE PIT AND THE PENDULUM

Impia tortorum longas hic turba furores
Sanguinis innocui, non satiata, aluit.
Sospite nunc patria, fracto nunc funeris antro,
Mors ubi dira fuit vita salusque patent.[27]
[Quatrain composed for the gates of a market to be
erected upon the site of the Jacobin Club House at
Paris.]

I was sick — sick unto death with that long agony; and when they at length unbound me,

___

27 *Impia . . . patent* — Here the impious mob, unsated,
nourished / The torturers' long orgies of shedding innocent
blood. / Now that the country is safe, now that the funeral
tumbril is shattered, / where there was horrible death, life
and health are seen.

and I was permitted to sit, I felt that my senses were leaving me. The sentence — the dread sentence of death — was the last of distinct accentuation which reached my ears. After that, the sound of the inquisitorial voices seemed merged in one dreamy indeterminate hum. It conveyed to my soul the idea of *revolution* — perhaps from its association in fancy with the burr of a mill-wheel. This only for a brief period, for presently I heard no more. Yet, for awhile, I saw — but with how terrible an exaggeration! I saw the lips of the black-robed judges. They appeared to me white — whiter than the sheet upon which I trace these words — and thin even to grotesqueness; thin with the intensity of their expression of firmness — of immovable resolution — of stern contempt of human torture. I saw that the decrees of what to me was Fate were still issuing from those lips. I saw them writhe with a deadly locution. I saw them fashion the syllables of my name; and I shuddered because no sound succeeded. I saw, too, for a few moments of delirious horror, the soft and nearly imperceptible waving of the sable draperies which enwrapped the walls of the apartment. And then my vision fell upon the seven tall candles upon the table. At first they wore the aspect of charity, and seemed white slender angels who would save me; but then, all at once, there came a most deadly nausea over my spirit, and I felt every fibre in my frame thrill as if I had touched the wire of a galvanic battery, while the angel forms became meaningless spectres, with heads of flame, and I saw that from them there would be no help. And then there stole into my fancy, like a rich musical note, the thought of what sweet rest there must be in the grave. The thought came gently and stealthily, and it seemed long before it attained full appreciation; but just as my spirit came at length properly to feel and entertain it, the figures of the judges vanished, as if magically, from before me; the tall candles sank into nothingness; their flames went out utterly; the blackness of darkness supervened; all sensations appeared swallowed up in a mad rushing descent as of the soul into Hades. Then silence, and stillness, and night were the universe.

I had swooned; but still will not say that all of consciousness was lost. What of it there remained I will not attempt to define, or even to describe; yet all was not lost. In the deepest slumber — no! In delirium — no! In a swoon — no! In death — no! even in the grave all *is not* lost. Else there is no immortality for man. Arousing from the most profound of slumbers, we break the gossamer web of *some* dream. Yet in a second afterward (so frail may that web have been) we remember not that we have dreamed. In the return to life from the swoon there are two stages: first, that of the sense of mental or spiritual; second, that of the sense of physical, existence. It seems probable that if, upon reaching the second stage, we could recall the impressions of the first, we should find these impressions eloquent in memories of the gulf beyond. And that gulf is — what? How at least shall we distinguish its shadows from those of the tomb? But if the impressions of what I have termed the first stage are not, at will, recalled, yet, after long interval, do they not come unbidden, while we marvel whence they come? He who has never swooned, is not he who finds strange palaces and wildly familiar faces in coals that glow; is not he who beholds floating in midair the sad visions that the many may not view; is not he who ponders over the perfume of some novel flower; is not he whose brain grows bewildered with the meaning of some musical cadence which has never before arrested his attention.

Amid frequent and thoughtful endeavors to remember, amid earnest struggles to regather some token of the state of seeming nothingness into which my soul had lapsed, there have been moments when I have dreamed of success; there have been brief, very brief periods when I have conjured up remembrances which the lucid reason of a later epoch assures me could have reference only to that condition of seeming unconsciousness. These shadows of memory tell, indistinctly, of tall figures that lifted and bore me in silence down — down — still down — till a hideous dizziness oppressed me at the mere idea of the interminableness of the descent. They tell also of a vague horror at my heart, on account of that heart's unnatural stillness. Then comes a sense of sudden motionlessness throughout all things; as if those who bore me (a ghastly train!) had outrun, in their descent, the limits of the limitless, and paused from the wearisomeness of their toil. After this I call to mind flatness and dampness; and then all is *madness* — the madness of a memory which busies itself among forbidden things.

Very suddenly there came back to my soul motion and sound — the tumultuous motion of the heart and, in my ears, the sound of its beating. Then a pause in which all is blank. Then again sound, and motion, and touch — a tingling sensation pervading my frame. Then the mere consciousness of existence, without thought — a condition which lasted long. Then, very suddenly, *thought,* and shuddering terror, and earnest endeavor to comprehend my true state. Then a strong desire to lapse into insensibility. Then a rushing revival of soul and a successful effort to move. And now a full memory of the trial, of the judges, of the sable draperies, of the sentence, of the sickness, of the swoon. Then entire forgetfulness of all that followed; of all that a later day and much earnestness of endeavor have enabled me vaguely to recall.

So far, I had not opened my eyes. I felt that I lay upon my back, unbound. I reached out my hand, and it fell heavily upon something damp and hard. There I suffered it to remain for many minutes, while I strove to imagine where and *what* I could be. I longed, yet dared not, to employ my vision. I dreaded the first glance at ob-

jects around me. It was not that I feared to look
upon things horrible, but that I grew aghast
lest there should be *nothing* to see. At length,
with a wild desperation at heart, I quickly un-
closed my eyes. My worst thoughts, then, were
confirmed. The blackness of eternal night encompassed me. I struggled for breath. The intensity of the darkness seemed to oppress and
stifle me. The atmosphere was intolerably close.
I still lay quietly, and made effort to exercise my
reason. I brought to mind the inquisitorial proceedings, and attempted from that point to de-
duce my real condition. The sentence had
passed; and it appeared to me that a very long
interval of time had since elapsed. Yet not for a
moment did I suppose myself actually dead.
Such a supposition, notwithstanding what we
read in fiction, is altogether inconsistent with
real existence; but where and in what state was
I? The condemned to death, I knew, perished
usually at the *auto-da-fés*,[28] and one of these had
been held on the very night of the day of my
trial. Had I been remanded to my dungeon, to
await the next sacrifice, which would not take
place for many months? This I at once saw
could not be. Victims had been in immediate
demand. Moreover, my dungeon, as well as all

[28] *auto-da-fés* — the ceremony accompanying the pro-
nouncement of sentence by the Inquisition and followed
by the execution of a punishment by the secular authori-
ties; especially the burning of a person condemned as a
heretic.

the condemned cells at Toledo,[29] had stone floors, and light was not altogether excluded.

A fearful idea now suddenly drove the blood in torrents upon my heart, and for a brief period I once more relapsed into insensibility. Upon recovering, I at once started to my feet, trembling convulsively in every fibre. I thrust my arms wildly above and around me in all directions. I felt nothing; yet dreaded to move a step, lest I should be impeded by the walls of a *tomb*. Perspiration burst from every pore, and stood in cold big beads upon my forehead. The agony of suspense grew at length intolerable, and I cautiously moved forward, with my arms extended, and my eyes straining from their sockets in the hope of catching some faint ray of light. I proceeded for many paces; but still all was blackness and vacancy. I breathed more freely. It seemed evident that mine was not, at least, the most hideous of fates.

And now, as I still continued to step cautiously onward, there came thronging upon my recollection a thousand vague rumors of the horrors of Toledo. Of the dungeons there had been strange things narrated — fables I had always deemed them — but yet strange, and too ghastly to repeat, save in a whisper. Was I left to perish of starvation in this subterranean

29 Toledo — a province in Spain, today existing in the area of New Castile. Although there is a long history of religious persecution and inquistion in Spain (especially in the 1400's when nonbelievers were converted, slain, or exiled) there is no factual evidence of the type of persecution Poe describes here.

world of darkness; or what fate, perhaps even more fearful, awaited me? That the result would be death, and a death of more than customary bitterness, I knew too well the character of my judges to doubt. The mode and the hour were all that occupied or distracted me.

My outstretched hands at length encountered some solid obstruction. It was a wall, seemingly of stone masonry — very smooth, slimy, and cold. I followed it up; stepping with all the careful distrust with which certain antique narratives had inspired me. This process, however, afforded me no means of ascertaining the dimensions of my dungeon, as I might make its circuit and return to the point whence I set out without being aware of the fact, so perfectly uniform seemed the wall. I therefore sought the knife which had been in my pocket when led into the inquisitorial chamber; but it was gone; my clothes had been exchanged for a wrapper of coarse serge. I had thought of forcing the blade in some minute crevice of the masonry, so as to identify my point of departure. The difficulty, nevertheless, was but trivial; although, in the disorder of my fancy, it seemed at first insuperable. I tore a part of the hem from the robe and placed the fragment at full length, and at right angles to the wall. In groping my way around the prison, I could not fail to encounter this rag upon completing the circuit. So, at least, I thought; but I had not counted upon the extent of the dungeon, or upon my own weakness. The

ground was moist and slippery. I staggered onward for some time, when I stumbled and fell.
My excessive fatigue induced me to remain
prostrate; and sleep soon overtook me as I lay.

Upon awaking, and stretching forth an arm,
I found beside me a loaf and a pitcher with
water. I was too much exhausted to reflect upon this circumstance, but ate and drank with
avidity. Shortly afterward, I resumed my tour
around the prison, and with much toil, came at
last upon the fragment of the serge. Up to the
period when I fell, I had counted fifty-two
paces, and, upon resuming my walk, I had
counted forty-eight more — when I arrived at the
rag. There were in all, then, a hundred paces;
and, admitting two paces to the yard, I pre-
sumed the dungeon to be fifty yards in circuit.
I had met, however, with many angles in the
wall, and thus I could form no guess at the shape
of the vault, for vault I could not help supposing it to be.

I had little object — certainly no hope — in
these researches; but a vague curiosity
prompted me to continue them. Quitting the
wall, I resolved to cross the area of the enclosure. At first, I proceeded with extreme caution,
for the floor, although seemingly of solid material, was treacherous with slime. At length, however, I took courage, and did not hesitate to
step firmly — endeavoring to cross in as direct a
line as possible. I had advanced some ten or
twelve paces in this manner, when the remnant

of the torn hem of my robe became entangled between my legs. I stepped on it, and fell violently on my face.

In the confusion attending my fall, I did not immediately apprehend a somewhat startling circumstance, which yet, in a few seconds afterward, and while I still lay prostrate, arrested my attention. It was this: My chin rested upon the floor of the prison, but my lips, and the upper portion of my head, although seemingly at a less elevation than the chin, touched nothing. At the same time, my forehead seemed bathed in a clammy vapor, and the peculiar smell of decayed fungus arose to my nostrils. I put forward my arm, and shuddered to find that I had fallen at the very brink of a circular pit, whose extent, of course, I had no means of ascertaining at the moment. Groping about the masonry just below the margin, I succeeded in dislodging a small fragment, and let it fall into the abyss. For many seconds I hearkened to its reverberations as it dashed against the sides of the chasm in its descent; at length, there was a sullen plunge into water, succeeded by loud echoes. At the same moment, there came a sound resembling the quick opening and as rapid closing of a door overhead, while a faint gleam of light flashed suddenly through the gloom, and as suddenly faded away.

I saw clearly the doom which had been prepared for me, and congratulated myself upon the timely accident by which I had escaped.

Another step before my fall, and the world had seen me no more. And the death just avoided was of that very character which I had regarded as fabulous and frivolous in the tales respecting the Inquisition. To the victims of its tyranny, there was the choice of death with its direst physical agonies, or death with its most hideous moral horrors. I had been reserved for the latter. By long suffering my nerves had been unstrung, until I trembled at the sound of my own voice, and had become in every respect a fitting subject for the species of torture which awaited me.

Shaking in every limb, I groped my way back to the wall — resolving there to perish rather than risk the terrors of the wells, of which my imagination now pictured many in various positions about the dungeon. In other conditions of mind, I might have had courage to end my misery at once, by a plunge into one of these abysses; but now I was the veriest of cowards. Neither could I forget what I had read of these pits — that the *sudden* extinction of life formed no part of their most horrible plan.

Agitation of spirit kept me awake for many long hours, but at length I again slumbered. Upon arousing, I found by my side, as before, a loaf and a pitcher of water. A burning thirst consumed me, and I emptied the vessel at a draught. It must have been drugged — for scarcely had I drunk, before I became irresistibly drowsy. A deep sleep fell upon me — a sleep like that of death. How long it lasted, of

course I know not; but when, once again, I un-
closed my eyes, the objects around me were
visible. By a wild, sulphurous lustre, the origin
of which I could not at first determine, I was
enabled to see the extent and aspect of the
prison.

In its size I had been greatly mistaken. The
whole circuit of its walls did not exceed twenty-
five yards. For some minutes this fact occasioned
me a world of vain trouble; vain indeed — for
what could be of less importance, under the
terrible circumstances which environed me,
than the mere dimensions of my dungeon? But
my soul took a wild interest in trifles, and I
busied myself in endeavors to account for the
error I had committed in my measurement. The
truth at length flashed upon me. In my first
attempt at exploration I had counted fifty-two
paces, up to the period when I fell: I must then
have been within a pace or two of the fragment
of serge; in fact, I had nearly performed the
circuit of the vault. I then slept — and, upon
awaking, I must have returned upon my steps
— thus supposing the circuit nearly double what
it actually was. My confusion of mind prevented
me from observing that I began my tour with
the wall to the right.

I had been deceived, too, in respect to the
shape of the enclosure. In feeling my way I had
found many angles, and thus deduced an idea of
great irregularity; so potent is the effect of total
darkness upon one arousing from lethargy or
sleep! The angles were simply those of a few

slight depressions, or niches, at odd intervals. The general shape of the prison was square. What I had taken for masonry seemed now to be iron, or some other metal, in huge plates, whose sutures or joints occasioned the depression. The entire surface of this metallic enclosure was rudely daubed in all the hideous and repulsive devices to which the charnel superstition of the monks has given rise. The figures of fiends in aspects of menace, with skeleton forms, and other more really fearful images, overspread and disfigured the walls. I observed that the outlines of these monstrosities were sufficiently distinct, but that the colors seemed faded and blurred, as if from the effects of a damp atmosphere. I now noticed the floor, too, which was of stone. In the centre yawned the circular pit from whose jaws I had escaped; but it was the only one in the dungeon.

All this I saw indistinctly and by much effort — for my personal condition had been greatly changed during slumber. I now lay upon my back, and at full length, on a species of low framework of wood. To this I was securely bound by a long strap resembling a surcingle. It passed in many convolutions about my limbs and body, leaving at liberty only my head, and my left arm to such extent, that I could, by dint of much exertion, supply myself with food from an earthen dish which lay by my side on the floor. I saw, to my horror, that the pitcher had been removed. I say to my horror — for I was consumed with intolerable thirst. This thirst it appeared to be the design of my persecutors to stimulate — for the food in the dish was meat pungently seasoned.

Looking upward, I surveyed the ceiling of my prison. It was some thirty or forty feet overhead, and constructed much as the side walls. In one of its panels a very singular figure riveted my whole attention. It was the painted figure of Time as he is commonly represented, save that, in lieu of a scythe, he held what, at a casual glance, I supposed to be the picture image of a huge pendulum, such as we see on antique clocks. There was something, however, in the appearance of this machine which caused me to regard it more attentively. While I gazed directly upward at it (for its position was immediately over my own) I fancied that I saw it in motion. In an instant afterward the fancy was confirmed. Its sweep was brief, and of course slow. I watched it for some minutes somewhat in fear, but more in wonder. Wearied at length with observing its dull movement, I turned my eyes upon the other objects in the cell.

A slight noise attracted my notice, and, looking to the floor, I saw several enormous rats traversing it. They had issued from the well which lay just within view to my right. Even then, while I gazed, they came up in troops, hurriedly, with ravenous eyes, allured by the scent of the meat. From this it required much effort and attention to scare them away.

It might have been half an hour, perhaps even an hour (for I could take but imperfect note of time), before I again cast my eyes upward. What I then saw confounded and amazed me. The sweep of the pendulum had increased in extent by nearly a yard. As a natural consequence its velocity was also much greater. But what mainly disturbed me was the idea that it had perceptibly *descended*. I now observed — with what horror it is needless to say — that its nether extremity was formed of a crescent of glittering steel, about a foot in length from horn to horn; the horns upward, and the under edge evidently as keen as that of a razor. Like a razor also, it seemed massy and heavy, tapering from the edge into a solid and broad structure above. It was appended to a weighty rod of brass, and the whole *hissed* as it swung through the air.

I could no longer doubt the doom prepared for me by monkish ingenuity in torture. My cognizance of the pit had become known to the inquisitorial agents — *the pit,* whose horrors had been destined for so bold a recusant [30] as myself — *the pit,* typical of hell and regarded by rumor as the Ultima Thule of all their punishments. The plunge into this pit I had avoided by the merest of accidents, and I knew that surprise, or entrapment into torment, formed an important portion of all the grotesqueries of these dungeon deaths. Having failed to fall, it was no part

[30] recusant — one who refuses to accept or obey established authority; a dissenter, a nonconformist.

of the demon plan to hurl me into the abyss, and thus (there being no alternative) a different and a milder destruction awaited me. Milder! I half smiled in my agony as I thought of such application of such a term.

What boots it to tell of the long, long hours of horror more than mortal, during which I counted the rushing oscillations of the steel! Inch by inch — line by line — with a descent only appreciable at intervals that seemed ages — down and still down it came! Days passed — it might have been that many days passed — ere it swept so closely over me as to fan me with its acrid breath. The odor of the sharp steel forced itself into my nostrils. I prayed — I wearied heaven with my prayer for its more speedy descent. I grew frantically mad, and struggled to force myself upward against the sweep of the fearful scimitar. And then I fell suddenly calm, and lay smiling at the glittering death, as a child at some rare bauble.

There was another interval of utter insensibility; it was brief; for, upon again lapsing into life, there had been no perceptible descent in the pendulum. But it might have been long — for I knew there were demons who took note of my swoon, and who could have arrested the vibration at pleasure. Upon my recovery, too, I felt very — oh! inexpressibly — sick and weak, as if through long inanition.[31] Even amid the agonies of that period, the human nature craved

---

[31] inanition — a condition arising from lack of food or water; lethargy.

food. With painful effort I outstretched my left arm as far as my bonds permitted, and took possession of the small remnant which had been spared me by the rats. As I put a portion of it within my lips, there rushed to my mind a half-formed thought of joy — of hope. Yet what business had *I* with hope? It was, as I say, a half formed thought — man has many such, which are never completed. I felt that it was of joy — of hope; but I felt also that it had perished in its formation. In vain I struggled to perfect — to regain it. Long suffering had nearly annihilated all my ordinary powers of mind. I was an imbecile — an idiot.

The vibration of the pendulum was at right angles to my length. I saw that the crescent was designed to cross the region of the heart. It would fray the serge of my robe — it would return and repeat its operations — again — and again. Notwithstanding its terrifically wide sweep (some thirty feet or more), and the hissing vigor of its descent, sufficient to sunder these very walls of iron, still the fraying of my robe would be all that, for several minutes, it would accomplish. And at this thought I paused. I dared not go further than this reflection. I dwelt upon it with a pertinacity of attention — as if, in so dwelling, I could arrest *here* the descent of the steel. I forced myself to ponder upon the sound of the crescent as it should pass across the garment — upon the peculiar thrilling sensation which the friction of cloth produces on the nerves. I pondered upon all this frivolity until my teeth were on edge.

Down — steadily down it crept. I took a frenzied pleasure in contrasting its downward with its lateral velocity. To the right — to the left — far and wide — with the shriek of a damned spirit! to my heart, with the stealthy pace of the tiger! I alternately laughed and howled, as the one or the other idea grew predominate.

Down — certainly, relentlessly down! It vibrated within three inches of my bosom! I struggled violently — furiously — to free my left arm. This was free only from the elbow to the hand. I could reach the latter, from the platter beside me, to my mouth, with great effort, but no farther. Could I have broken the fastenings above the elbow, I would have seized and attempted to arrest the pendulum. I might as well have attempted to arrest an avalanche!

Down — still unceasingly — still inevitably down! I gasped and struggled at each vibration. I shrunk convulsively at its every sweep. My eyes followed its outward or upward whirls with the eagerness of the most unmeaning despair; they closed themselves spasmodically at the descent, although death would have been a relief, oh, how unspeakable! Still I quivered in every nerve to think how slight a sinking of the machinery would precipitate that keen, glistening axe upon my bosom. It was *hope* that prompted the nerve to quiver — the frame to shrink. It was *hope* — the hope that triumphs on the rack —

that whispers to the death-condemned even in the dungeons of the Inquisition.

I saw that some ten or twelve vibrations would bring the steel in actual contact with my robe — and with this observation there suddenly came over my spirit all the keen, collected calmness of despair. For the first time during many hours — or perhaps days — I *thought*. It now occurred to me that the bandage, or surcingle, which enveloped me, was *unique*. I was tied by no separate cord. The first stroke of the razorlike crescent athwart any portion of the band would so detach it that it might be unwound from my person by means of my left hand. But how fearful, in that case, the proximity of the steel! Was it likely, moreover, that the minions of the torturer had not foreseen and provided for this possibility? Was it probable that the bandage crossed my bosom in the track of the pendulum? Dreading to find my faint and, as it seemed, my last hope frustrated, I so far elevated my head as to obtain a distinct view of my breast. The surcingle enveloped my limbs and body close in all directions — *save in the path of the destroying crescent*.

Scarcely had I dropped my head back into its original position, when there flashed upon my mind what I cannot better describe than as the unformed half of that idea of deliverance to which I have previously alluded, and of which a moiety only floated indeterminately through my brain when I raised food to my burning lips.

The whole thought was now present — feeble, scarcely sane, scarcely definite — but still entire. I proceeded at once, with the nervous energy of despair, to attempt its execution.

For many hours the immediate vicinity of the low framework upon which I lay had been literally swarming with rats. They were wild, bold, ravenous — their red eyes glaring upon me as if they waited but for motionlessness on my part to make me their prey. "To what food," I thought, "have they been accustomed in the well?"

They had devoured, in spite of all my efforts to prevent them, all but a small remnant of the contents of the dish. I had fallen into an habitual see-saw or wave of the hand about the platter; and, at length, the unconscious uniformity of the movement deprived it of effect. In their voracity, the vermin frequently fastened their sharp fangs in my fingers. With the particles of the oily and spicy viand which now remained, I thoroughly rubbed the bandage wherever I could reach it; then, raising my hand from the floor, I lay breathlessly still.

At first, the ravenous animals were startled and terrified at the change — at the cessation of movement. They shrank alarmedly back; many sought the well. But this was only for a moment. I had not counted in vain upon their voracity. Observing that I remained without motion, one or two of the boldest leaped upon the framework, and smelt at the surcingle. This seemed the signal for a general rush. Forth from the well they hurried in fresh troops. They clung to the wood — they overran it, and leaped in hundreds upon my person. The measured movement of the pendulum disturbed them not at all. Avoiding its strokes, they busied themselves with the anointed bandage. They pressed — they swarmed upon me in ever accumulating heaps. They writhed upon my throat; their cold lips sought my own; I was half stifled by their thronging pressure; disgust, for which the world has no name, swelled my bosom, and chilled, with a heavy clamminess, my heart. Yet one minute, and I felt that the struggle would be over. Plainly I perceived the loosening of the bandage. I knew that in more than one place it must be already severed. With a more than human resolution I lay *still*.

Nor had I erred in my calculations — nor had I endured in vain. I at length felt that I was *free*. The surcingle hung in ribands from my body. But the stroke of the pendulum already pressed upon my bosom. It had divided the serge of the robe. It had cut through the linen beneath. Twice again it swung, and a sharp sense of pain shot through every nerve. But the moment of escape had arrived. At a wave of my hand my deliverers hurried tumultuously away. With a steady movement — cautious, sidelong, shrinking, and slow — I slid from the embrace of the bandage and beyond the reach of the scimitar. For the moment, at least, *I was free.*

Free! — and in the grasp of the Inquisition! I had scarcely stepped from my wooden bed of horror upon the stone floor of the prison, when the motion of the hellish machine ceased, and I beheld it drawn up, by some invisible force, through the ceiling. This was a lesson which I took desperately to heart. My every motion was undoubtedly watched. Free! — I had but escaped death in one form of agony, to be delivered unto worse than death in some other. With that thought I rolled my eyes nervously around on the barriers of iron that hemmed me in. Something unusual — some change which, at first, I could not appreciate distinctly — it was obvious, had taken place in the apartment. For many minutes of a dreamy and trembling abstraction, I busied myself in vain, unconnected conjecture. During this period, I became aware, for the first time, of the origin of the sulphurous light which illumined the cell. It proceeded from a fissure, about half an inch in width, extending entirely around the prison at the base of the walls, which it thus appeared were completely separated from the floor. I endeavored, but of course in vain, to look through the aperture.

As I arose from the attempt, the mystery of the alteration in the chamber broke at once upon my understanding. I have observed that, although the outlines of the figures upon the walls were sufficiently distinct, yet the colors seemed blurred and indefinite. These colors had now assumed, and were momentarily assuming, a startling and most intense brilliancy, that gave to the spectral and fiendish portraitures an aspect that might have thrilled even firmer nerves than my own. Demon eyes, of a wild and ghastly vivacity, glared upon me in a thousand directions, where none had been visible before, and gleamed with the lurid lustre of a fire that I could not force my imagination to regard as unreal.

Unreal! — Even while I breathed there came to my nostrils the breath of the vapor of heated iron! A suffocating odor pervaded the prison! A deeper glow settled each moment in the eyes that glared at my agonies! A richer tint of crimson diffused itself over the pictured horrors of blood. I panted! I gasped for breath! There could be no doubt of the design of my tormentors — oh! most unrelenting! oh! most demoniac of men! I shrank from the glowing metal to the centre of the cell. Amid the thought of the fiery destruction that impended, the idea of the coolness of the well came over my soul like balm. I rushed to its deadly brink. I threw my straining vision below. The glare from the enkindled roof illumined its inmost recesses. Yet, for a wild moment, did my spirit refuse to comprehend the meaning of what I saw. At length it forced — it wrestled its way into my soul — it burned itself in upon my shuddering reason. Oh! for a voice to speak! — oh! horror! — oh! any horror but this! With a shriek, I rushed from the margin, and buried my face in my hands — weeping bitterly.

The heat rapidly increased, and once again I looked up, shuddering as with a fit of ague. There had been a second change in the cell — and now the change was obviously in the *form*. As before, it was in vain that I at first endeavored to appreciate or understand what was taking place. But not long was I left in doubt. The Inquisitorial vengeance had been hurried by my two-fold escape, and there was to be no more dallying with the King of Terrors. The room had been square. I saw that two of its iron angles were now acute — two, consequently, obtuse. The fearful difference quickly increased with a low rumbling or moaning sound. In an instant the apartment had shifted its form into that of a lozenge. But the alteration stopped not here — I neither hoped nor desired it to stop. I could have clasped the red walls to my bosom as a garment of eternal peace. "Death," I said, "any death but that of the pit!" Fool! might I not have known that *into the pit* it was the object of the burning iron to urge me? Could I resist its glow? or if even that, could I withstand its pressure? And now, flatter and flatter grew the lozenge, with a rapidity that left me no time for contemplation. Its centre, and of course its greatest width, came just over the yawning gulf. I shrank back — but the closing walls pressed me resistlessly onward. At length for my seared and writhing body there was no longer an inch of foothold on the firm floor of the prison. I struggled no more, but the agony of my soul found vent in one loud, long, and final scream of despair. I felt that I tottered upon the brink — I averted my eyes —

There was a discordant hum of human voices! There was a loud blast as of many trumpets! There was a harsh grating as of a thousand thunders! The fiery walls rushed back! An outstretched arm caught my own as I fell, fainting, into the abyss. It was that of General Lasalle. The French army had entered Toledo. The Inquisition was in the hands of its enemies.

LIGEIA

And the will therein lieth, which dieth not. Who knoweth the mysteries of the will, with its vigor? For God is but a great will pervading all things by nature of its intentness. Man doth not yield himself to the angels, nor unto death utterly, save only through the weakness of his feeble will.

— *Joseph Glanvill*

I CANNOT, for my soul, remember how, when, or even precisely where I first became acquainted with the Lady Ligeia. Long years have since elapsed, and my memory is feeble through much suffering. Or, perhaps, I cannot *now* bring these points to mind, because, in truth, the character of my beloved, her rare learning, her singular yet placid cast of beauty, and the thrilling and enthralling eloquence of her low musical language, made their way into my heart by paces so steadily and stealthily progressive that they have been unnoticed and unknown. Yet I believe that I met her first and most frequently in some large, old, decaying city near the Rhine. Of her family — I have surely heard her speak. That it is of a remotely ancient date cannot be doubted. Ligeia! Ligeia! Buried in studies of a nature more than all else adapted to deaden impressions of the outward world, it is by that sweet word alone — by Ligeia — that I bring before mine eyes in fancy the image of her who is no more. And now, while I write, a recollection flashes upon me that I have *never known* the paternal name of her who was my friend and my betrothed, and who became the partner of my studies, and finally the wife of my bosom. Was it a playful charge on the part of my Ligeia? or was it a test of my strength of affection that I should institute no inquiries upon this point? or was it rather a caprice of my own — a wildly romantic offering on the shrine of the most passionate devotion? I but indistinctly recall the fact itself — what wonder that I have utterly forgotten the circumstances which originated or attended it? And, indeed, if ever that spirit which is entitled *Romance* — if ever she, the wan and the misty-winged *Ashtophet* [32] of idolatrous Egypt, presided, as they

32 Ashtophet — the Phoenician Astarte, goddess of fertility and sexual love.

tell, over marriages ill-omened, then most surely she presided over mine.

There is one dear topic, however, on which my memory fails me not. It is the *person* of Ligeia. In stature she was tall, somewhat slender, and, in her latter days, even emaciated. I would in vain attempt to portray the majesty, the quiet ease of her demeanor, or the incomprehensible lightness and elasticity of her footfall. She came and departed as a shadow. I was never made aware of her entrance into my closed study, save by the dear music of her low, sweet voice, as she placed her marble hand upon my shoulder. In beauty of face no maiden ever equaled her. It was the radiance of an opium dream — an airy and spirit-lifting vision more wildly divine than the phantasies which hovered about the slumbering souls of the daughters of Delos. Yet her features were not of that regular mold which we have been falsely taught to worship in the classical labors of the heathen. "There is no exquisite beauty," says Bacon, Lord Verulam, speaking truly of all the forms and *genera* of beauty, "without some *strangeness* in the proportion." Yet, although I saw that the features of Ligeia were not of a classic regularity — although I perceived that her loveliness was indeed "exquisite," and felt that there was much of "strangeness" pervading it, yet I have tried in vain to detect the irregularity and to trace home my own perception of "the strange." I examined the contour of the lofty and pale forehead — it was faultless — how cold indeed that word when applied to a majesty so divine — the skin rivaling the purest ivory, the commanding extent and repose, the gentle prominence of the regions above the temples; and then the raven-black, the glossy, the luxuriant, and naturally curling tresses, setting forth the full force of the Homeric epithet, "hyacinthine!" I looked at the delicate outlines of the nose — and nowhere but in the graceful medallions of the Hebrews had I beheld a similar perfection. There were the same luxurious smoothness of surface, the same scarcely perceptible tendency to the aquiline, the same harmoniously curved nostrils speaking the free spirit. I regarded the sweet mouth. Here was indeed the triumph of all things heavenly — the magnificent turn of the short upper lip — the soft, voluptuous slumber of the under — the dimples which sported, and the color which spoke — the teeth glancing back, with a brilliancy almost startling, every ray of the holy light which fell upon them in her serene and placid yet most exultingly radiant of all smiles. I scrutinized the formation of the chin — and, here too, I found the gentleness of breadth, the softness and the majesty, the fullness and the spirituality, of the Greek — the contour which the god Apollo revealed but in a dream, to Cleomenes, the son of the Athenian. And then I peered into the large eyes of Ligeia.

For eyes we have no models in the remotely

antique. It might have been, too, that in these
eyes of my beloved lay the secret to which Lord
Verulam alludes. They were, I must believe, far
larger than the ordinary eyes of our own race.
They were even fuller than the fullest of the
gazelle eyes of the tribe of the valley of Nourja-
had. Yet it was only at intervals — in moments
of intense excitement — that this peculiarity became more than slightly noticeable in Ligeia. And
at such moments was her beauty — in my heated
fancy thus it appeared perhaps — the beauty
of beings either above or apart from the
earth — the beauty of the fabulous Houri of the
Turk. The hue of the orbs was the most brilliant
of black, and, far over them, hung jetty lashes
of great length. The brows, slightly irregular in
outline, had the same tint. The "strangeness,"
however, which I found in the eyes was of a
nature distinct from the formation, or the color,
or the brilliancy of the features, and must, after
all, be referred to the *expression*. Ah, word of
no meaning! behind whose vast latitude of mere
sound we entrench our ignorance of so much of
the spiritual. The expression of the eyes of
Ligeia! How for long hours have I pondered upon it! How have I, through the whole of a mid-
summer night, struggled to fathom it! What was
it — that something more profound than the
well of Democritus — which lay far within the
pupils of my beloved? What *was* it? I was possessed with a passion to discover. Those eyes!
those large, those shining, those divine orbs!

they became to me twin stars of Leda, and I to them devoutest of astrologers.

There is no point, among the many incomprehensible anomalies of the science of mind, more thrillingly exciting than the fact — never, I believe, noticed in the schools — that in our endeavors to recall to memory something long forgotten, we often find ourselves *upon the very verge* of remembrance, without being able, in the end, to remember. And thus how frequently, in my intense scrutiny of Ligeia's eyes, have I felt approaching the full knowledge of their expression — felt it approaching — yet not quite be mine — and so at length entirely depart! And (strange, oh, strangest mystery of all!) I found, in the commonest objects of the universe, a circle of analogies to that expression. I mean to say that, subsequent to the period when Ligeia's beauty passed into my spirit, there dwelling as in a shrine, I derived, from many existences in the material world, a sentiment such as I felt always around, within me, by her large and luminous orbs. Yet not the more could I define that sentiment, or analyze, or even steadily view it. I recognized it, let me repeat, sometimes in the survey of a rapidly growing vine — in the contemplation of a moth, a butterfly, a chrysalis, a stream of running water. I have felt it in the ocean — in the falling of a meteor. I have felt it in the glances of unusually aged people. And there are one or two stars in heaven (one especially, a star of the sixth magnitude, double and

changeable, to be found near the large star in
Lyra) in a telescopic scrutiny of which I have
been made aware of the feeling. I have been
filled with it by certain sounds from stringed
instruments, and not unfrequently by passages
from books. Among innumerable other in-
stances, I well remember something in a volume
of Joseph Glanvill, which (perhaps merely
from its quaintness — who shall say?) never
failed to inspire me with the sentiment: "And
the will therein lieth, which dieth not. Who
knoweth the mysteries of the will, with its vigor?
For God is but a great will pervading all things
by nature of its intentness. Man doth not yield
him to the angels, nor unto death utterly, save
only through the weakness of his feeble will."

Length of years and subsequent reflection
have enabled me to trace, indeed, some remote
connection between this passage in the English
moralist and a portion of the character of
Ligeia. An *intensity* in thought, action, or
speech was possibly, in her, a result, or at least
an index, of that gigantic volition which, during
our long intercourse, failed to give other and
more immediate evidence of its existence. Of
all the women whom I have ever known, she,
the outwardly calm, the ever-placid Ligeia, was
the most violently a prey to the tumultuous vul-
tures of stern passion. And of such passion I
could form no estimate, save by the miraculous expansion of those eyes which at once so
delighted and appalled me — by the almost magi-

cal melody, modulation, distinctness, and placidity of her very low voice — and by the fierce
energy (rendered doubly effective by contrast
with her manner of utterance) of the wild
words which she habitually uttered.

I have spoken of the learning of Ligeia: It
was immense — such as I have never known in
woman. In the classical tongues was she deeply
proficient, and as far as my own acquaintance
extended in regard to the modern dialects of
Europe, I have never known her at fault. Indeed upon any theme of the most admired because simply the most abstruse of the boasted
erudition of the Academy, have I *ever* found
Ligeia at fault? How singularly — how thrillingly, this one point in the nature of my wife
has forced itself, at this late period only, upon
my attention! I said her knowledge was such as
I have never known in woman — but where
breathes the man who has traversed, and successfully, *all* the wide areas of moral, physical,
and mathematical science? I saw not then
what I now clearly perceive, that the acquisi-
tions of Ligeia were gigantic, were astounding;
yet I was sufficiently aware of her infinite su-
premacy to resign myself, with a childlike confidence, to her guidance through the chaotic
world of metaphysical investigation at which I
was most busily occupied during the earlier
years of our marriage. With how vast a triumph
— with how vivid a delight — with how much of
all that is ethereal in hope did I *feel*, as she bent

over me in studies but little sought, but less known — that delicious vista by slow degrees expanding before me, down whose long, gorgeous, and all untrodden path I might at length pass onward to the goal of a wisdom too divinely precious not to be forbidden!

How poignant, then, must have been the grief with which, after some years, I beheld my well-grounded expectations take wings to themselves and fly away! Without Ligeia I was but as a child groping benighted. Her presence, her readings alone, rendered vividly luminous the many mysteries of the transcendentalism in which we were immersed. Wanting the radiant lustre of her eyes, letters, lambent and golden, grew duller than Saturnian lead. And now those eyes shone less and less frequently upon the pages over which I pored. Ligeia grew ill. The wild eyes blazed with a too — too glorious effulgence; the pale fingers became of the transparent waxen hue of the grave; and the blue veins upon the lofty forehead swelled and sank impetuously with the tides of the most gentle emotion. I saw that she must die — and I struggled desperately in spirit with the grim Azrael.[33] And the struggles of the passionate wife were, to my astonishment, even more energetic than my own. There had been much in her stern nature to impress me with the belief that, to her, death would have come without its terrors; but not so. Words are impotent to convey any just idea of the fierceness of resistance with which she wres-

[33] Azrael — the angel of death in Jewish and Islamic belief.

tled with the Shadow. I groaned in anguish at
the pitiable spectacle. I would have soothed —
I would have reasoned; but in the intensity of
her wild desire for life — for life — *but* for life —
solace and reason were alike the uttermost of
folly. Yet not until the last instance, amid the
most convulsive writhings of her fierce spirit,
was shaken the external placidity of her demeanor. Her voice grew more gentle — grew
more low — yet I would not wish to dwell upon
the wild meaning of the quietly uttered words.
My brain reeled as I hearkened, entranced to a
melody more than mortal — to assumptions
and aspirations which mortality had never before known.

That she loved me I should not have
doubted; and I might have been easily aware
that, in a bosom such as hers, love would have
reigned no ordinary passion. But in death only
was I fully impressed with the strength of her
affection. For long hours, detaining my hand,
would she pour out before me the overflowing
of a heart whose more than passionate devotion
amounted to idolatry. How had I deserved to be
so blessed by such confessions? How had I deserved to be so cursed with the removal of my
beloved in the hour of my making them? But
upon this subject I cannot bear to dilate. Let me
say only that, in Ligeia's more than womanly
abandonment to a love, alas! all unmerited, all
unworthily bestowed, I at length recognized the
principle of her longing, with so wildly earnest a

desire, for the life which was now fleeing so rapidly away. It is this wild longing — it is this eager vehemence of desire for life — *but* for life — that I have no power to portray — no utterance capable of expressing.

At high noon of the night in which she departed, beckoning me, peremptorily, to her side, she bade me repeat certain verses composed by herself not many days before. I obeyed her. They were these:

> Lo! 'tis a gala night
>   Within the lonesome latter years!
> An angel throng, bewinged, bedight
>   In veils, and drowned in tears,
> Sit in a theater to see
>   A play of hopes and fears,
> While the orchestra breathes fitfully
>   The music of the spheres.
>
> Mimes, in the form of God on high,
>   Mutter and mumble low,
> And hither and thither fly;
>   Mere puppets they, who come and go
>
> At bidding of vast formless things
>   That shift the scenery to and fro,
> Flapping from out their condon wings
>   Invisible Woe!
>
> That motley drama!—oh, be sure
>   It shall not be forgot!
> With its Phantom chased for evermore,
>   By a crowd that seize it not,
> Through a circle that ever returneth in
>   To the self-same spot;
> And much of Madness, and more of Sin
>   And Horror, the soul of the plot!
>
> But see, amid the mimic rout
>   A crawling shape intrude!
> A blood-red thing that writhes from out
>   The scenic solitude!

It writhes! — it writhes! — with mortal pangs
  The mimes become its food,
And the seraphs sob at vermin fangs
  In human gore imbued.

Out-out are the lights — out all!
  And over each quivering form,
The curtain, a funeral pall,
  Comes down with the rush of a storm —
And the angels, all pallid and wan,
  Uprising, unveiling, affirm
That the play is the tragedy, "Man,"
  And its hero, the conqueror Worm.

"O God!" half shrieked Ligeia, leaping to her
feet and extending her arms aloft with a spas-
modic movement, as I made an end of these
lines — "O God! O Divine Father! — shall these
things be undeviatingly so? — shall this conqueror be not once conquered? Are we not part
and parcel in Thee? Who — who knoweth the
mysteries of the will with its vigor? Man doth
not yield him to the angels, *nor unto death
utterly,* save only through the weakness of his
feeble will."

And now, as if exhausted with emotion, she
suffered her white arms to fall, and returned
solemnly to her bed of death. And as she
breathed her last sighs, there came mingled with
them a low murmur from her lips. I bent to
them my ear, and distinguished, again, the
concluding words of the passage in Glanvill:
*"Man doth not yield him to the angels, nor unto
death utterly, save only through the weakness
of his feeble will."*

She died: and I, crushed into the very dust

with sorrow, could no longer endure the lonely
desolation of my dwelling in the dim and decaying city by the Rhine. I had no lack of what
the world calls wealth. Ligeia had brought me
far more, very far more, than ordinarily falls to
the lot of mortals. After a few months, therefore, of weary and aimless wandering, I pur-
chased and put in some repair an abbey, which
I shall not name, in one of the wildest and least
frequented portions of fair England. The
gloomy and dreary grandeur of the building, the
almost savage aspect of the domain, the many
melancholy and time-honored memories connected with both, had much in unison with the
feelings of utter abandonment which had
driven me into that remote and unsocial region
of the country. Yet although the external abbey,
with its verdant decay hanging about it, suffered
but little alteration, I gave way, with a childlike perversity, and perchance with a faint hope
of alleviating my sorrows, to a display of more
than regal magnificance within. For such follies,
even in childhood, I had imbibed a taste, and
now they came back to me as if in the dotage
of grief. Alas, I feel how much even of incipient
madness might have been discovered in the gorgeous and fantastic draperies, in the solemn
carvings of Egypt, in the wild cornices and furniture, in the bedlam patterns of the carpets of
tufted gold! I had become a bounden slave in
the trammels of opium, and my labors and my
orders had taken a coloring from my dreams.

But these absurdities I must not pause to detail.
Let me speak only of that one chamber, ever
accursed, whither, in a moment of mental alien-
ation, I led from the altar as my bride — as the
successor of the unforgotten Ligeia — the fair-
haired and blue-eyed Lady Rowena Trevanion,
of Tremaine.

There is no individual portion of the archi-
tecture and decoration of that bridal chamber
which is not now visibly before me. Where were
the souls of the haughty family of the bride,
when, through thirst of gold, they permitted to
pass the threshold of an apartment *so* bedecked,
a maiden and a daughter so beloved? I have said
that I minutely remember the details of the
chamber — yet I am sadly forgetful on topics of
deep moment; and here there was no system, no
keeping, in the fantastic display, to take hold
upon the memory. The room lay in a high turret of the castellated abbey, was pentagonal in
shape, and of capacious size. Occupying the
whole southern face of the pentagon was the
sole window — an immense sheet of unbroken
glass from Venice — a single pane, and tinted of
a leaden hue, so that the rays of either the sun
or moon passing through it fell with a ghastly
lustre on the objects within. Over the upper
portion of this huge window extended the trelliswork of an aged vine, which clambered up
the mossy walls of the turret. The ceiling,
of gloomy-looking oak, was excessively lofty,
vaulted, and elaborately fretted with the wildest

and most grotesque specimens of a semi-Gothic,
semi-Druidical device. From out the most central
recess of this melancholy vaulting depended, by
a single chain of gold with long links, a huge
censer of the same metal, Saracenic in pattern,
and with many perforations so contrived that
there writhed in and out of them, as if endued
with a serpent vitality, a continual succession of
particolored fires.

Some few ottomans and golden candelabra,
of Eastern figure, were in various stations
about; and there was the couch, too — the
bridal couch — of an Indian model, and low,
and sculptured of solid ebony, with a pall-like
canopy above. In each of the angles of the chamber stood on end a gigantic sarcophagus of black
granite, from the tombs of the kings over against
Luxor, with their aged lids full of immemorial
sculpture. But in the draping of the apartment
lay, alas! the chief phantasy of all. The lofty
walls, gigantic in height — even unproportion-
ably so — were hung from summit to foot, in
vast folds, with a heavy and massive-looking
tapestry — tapestry of a material which was
found alike as a carpet on the floor, as a cover-
ing for the ottomans and the ebony bed, as a
canopy for the bed and as the gorgeous volutes
of the curtains which partially shaded the window. The material was the richest cloth of gold.
It was spotted all over, at irregular intervals,
with arabesque figures, about a foot in diameter,
and wrought upon the cloth in patterns of the

most jet black. But these figures partook of the
true character of the arabesque only when regarded from a single point of view. By a con-
trivance now common, and indeed traceable to
a very remote period of antiquity, they were
made changeable in aspect. To one entering
the room, they bore the appearance of simple
monstrosities; but upon a farther advance, this
appearance gradually departed; and, step by
step, as the visitor moved his station in the
chamber, he saw himself surrounded by an end-
less succession of the ghastly forms which belong
to the superstition of the Norman, or arise in
the guilty slumbers of the monk. The phantasmagoric effect was vastly heightened by the artificial introduction of a strong continual current
of wind behind the draperies — giving a hideous and uneasy animation to the whole.

In halls such as these — in a bridal chamber
such as this — I passed, with the Lady of Tremaine, the unhallowed hours of the first month
of our marriage — passed them with but little
disquietude. That my wife dreaded the fierce
moodiness of my temper — that she shunned me,
and loved me but little — I could not help perceiving; but it gave me rather pleasure than
otherwise. I loathed her with a hatred belonging
more to demon than to man. My memory flew
back (oh, with what intensity of regret!) to
Ligeia, the beloved, the august, the beautiful,
the entombed. I reveled in recollections of her
purity, of her wisdom, of her lofty — her ethe-

real nature, of her passionate, her idolatrous love. Now, then, did my spirit fully and freely burn with more than all the fires of her own. In the excitement of my opium dreams (for I was habitually fettered in the shackles of the drug), I would call aloud upon her name, during the silence of the night, or among the sheltered recesses of the glens by day, as if, through the wild eagerness, the solemn passion, the consuming ardor of my longing for the departed, I could restore her to the pathways she had abandoned — ah, *could* it be forever? — upon the earth.

About the commencement of the second month of the marriage, the Lady Rowena was attacked with sudden illness, from which her recovery was slow. The fever which consumed her rendered her nights uneasy; and in her perturbed state of half slumber, she spoke of sounds, and of motions, in and about the chamber of the turret, which I concluded had no origin save in the distemper of her fancy, or perhaps in the phantasmagoric influences of the chamber itself. She became at length convalescent — finally, well. Yet but a brief period elapsed, ere a second more violent disorder again threw her upon a bed of suffering; and from this attack her frame, at all times feeble, never altogether recovered. Her illnesses were, after this epoch, of alarming character and more alarming recurrence, defying alike the knowledge and the great exertions of her physicians. With the increase of the chronic disease, which had thus, apparently, taken too sure a hold upon her constitution to be eradicated by human means, I could not fail to observe a similar increase in the nervous irritation of her temperament, and in her excitability by trivial causes of fear. She spoke again, and now more frequently and pertinaciously, of the sounds — of the slight sounds — and of the unusual motions among the tapestries, to which she had formerly alluded.

One night, near the closing in of September, she pressed this distressing subject with more than usual emphasis upon my attention. She had just awakened from an unquiet slumber, and I had been watching, with feelings half of anxiety, half of vague terror, the workings of her emaciated countenance. I sat by the side of her ebony bed, upon one of the ottomans of India. She partly arose, and spoke, in an earnest low whisper, of sounds which she *then* heard, but which I could not hear — of motions which she *then* saw, but which I could not perceive. The wind was rushing hurriedly behind the tapestries, and I wished to show her (what, let me confess it, I could not *all* believe) that those almost inarticulate breathings, and those very gentle variations of the figures upon the wall, were but the natural effects of that customary rushing of the wind. But a deadly pallor, overspreading her face, had proved to me that my exertions to reassure her would be fruitless. She appeared to be fainting, and no attendants were within call.

I remembered where was deposited a decanter of light wine which had been ordered by her physicians, and hastened across the chamber to procure it. But, as I stepped beneath the light of the censer, two circumstances of a startling nature attracted my attention. I had felt that some palpable although invisible object had passed lightly by my person; and I saw that there lay upon the golden carpet, in the very middle of the rich lustre thrown from the censer, a shadow — a faint, indefinite shadow of angelic aspect — such as might be fancied for the shadow of a shade. But I was wild with the excitement of an immoderate dose of opium, and heeded these things but little, nor spoke of them to Rowena. Having found the wine, I recrossed the chamber, and poured out a gobletful, which I held to the lips of the fainting lady. She had now partially recovered, however, and took the vessel herself, while I sank upon an ottoman near me, with my eyes fastened upon her person. It was then that I became distinctly aware of a gentle footfall upon the carpet, and near the couch; and in a second thereafter, as Rowena was in the act of raising the wine to her lips, I saw, or may have dreamed that I saw, fall within the goblet, as if from some invisible spring in the atmosphere of the room, three or four large drops of a brilliant and ruby-colored fluid. If this I saw — not so Rowena. She swallowed the wine unhesitatingly, and I forbore to speak to her of a circumstance which must, after all, I considered, have been but the suggestion of a vivid imagination, rendered morbidly active by the terror of the lady, by the opium, and by the hour.

Yet I cannot conceal it from my own perception that, immediately subsequent to the fall of the ruby drops, a rapid change for the worse took place in the disorder of my wife; so that, on the third subsequent night, the hands of her menials prepared her for the tomb, and on the fourth, I sat alone, with her shrouded body, in that fantastic chamber which had received her as my bride. Wild visions, opium-engendered, flitted, shadowlike, before me. I gazed with unquiet eye upon the sarcophagi in the angles of the room, upon the varying figures of the drapery, and upon the writhing of the particolored fires in the censer overhead. My eyes then fell, as I called to mind the circumstances of a former night, to the spot beneath the glare of the censer where I had seen the faint traces of the shadow. It was there, however, no longer; and breathing with greater freedom, I turned my glances to the pallid and rigid figure upon the bed. Then rushed upon me a thousand memories of Ligeia — and then came back upon my heart, with the turbulent violence of a flood, the whole of that unutterable woe with which I had regarded *her* thus enshrouded. The night waned and still, with a bosom full of bitter thoughts of the one only and supremely beloved, I remained gazing upon the body of Rowena.

It might have been midnight, or perhaps

earlier or later, for I had taken no note of time, when a sob, low, gentle, but very distinct, startled me from my revery. I *felt* that it came from the bed of ebony — the bed of death. I listened in an agony of superstitious terror — but there was no repetition of the sound. I strained my vision to detect any motion in the corpse — but there was not the slightest perceptible. Yet I could not have been deceived. I *had* heard the noise, however faint, and my soul was awakened within me. I resolutely and perseveringly kept my attention riveted upon the body. Many minutes elapsed before any circumstance occurred tending to throw light upon the mystery. At length it became evident that a slight, a very feeble, and barely noticeable tinge of color had flushed up within the cheeks, and along the sunken small veins of the eyelids. Through a species of unutterable horror and awe, for which the language of mortality has no sufficiently energetic expression, I felt my heart cease to beat, my limbs grow rigid where I sat. Yet a sense of duty finally operated to restore my self-possession. I could no longer doubt that we had been precipitate in our preparations — that Rowena still lived. It was necessary that some immediate exertion be made; yet the turret was altogether apart from the portion of the abbey tenanted by the servants — there were none within call — I had no means of summoning them to my aid without leaving the room for many minutes — and this I could not venture to

do. I therefore struggled alone in my endeavors
to call back the spirit still hovering. In a short
period it was certain, however, that a relapse
had taken place; the color disappeared from
both eyelid and cheek, leaving a wanness even
more than that of marble; the lips became
doubly shriveled and pinched up in the ghastly
expression of death; a repulsive clamminess and
coldness overspread rapidly the surface of the
body; and all the usual rigorous stiffness immediately supervened. I fell back with a shudder
upon the couch from which I had been so star-
tlingly aroused, and again gave myself up to passionate waking visions of Ligeia.

An hour thus elapsed, when (could it be possible?) I was a second time aware of some vague
sound issuing from the region of the bed. I listened — in extremity of horror. The sound came
again — it was a sigh. Rushing to the corpse, I
saw — distinctly saw — a tremor upon the lips.
In a minute afterward they relaxed, disclosing a
bright line of the pearly teeth. Amazement now
struggled in my bosom with the profound awe
which had hitherto reigned there alone. I felt
that my vision grew dim, that my reason wan-
dered; and it was only by a violent effort that I
at length succeeded in nerving myself to the
task which duty thus once more had pointed out.
There was now a partial glow upon the forehead and upon the cheek and throat; a perceptible warmth pervaded the whole frame;
there was even a slight pulsation at the heart.

The lady *lived;* and with redoubled ardor I betook myself to the task of restoration. I chafed and bathed the temples and the hands, and used every exertion which experience, and no little medical reading, could suggest. But in vain. Suddenly, the color fled, the pulsation ceased, the lips resumed the expression of the dead, and, in an instant afterward, the whole body took upon itself the icy chilliness, the livid hue, the intense rigidity, the sunken outline, and all the loathsome peculiarities of that which has been, for many days, a tenant of the tomb.

And again I sunk into visions of Ligeia — and again (what marvel that I shudder while I write?), *again* there reached my ears a low sob from the region of the ebony bed. But why shall I minutely detail the unspeakable horrors of that night? Why shall I pause to relate how, time after time, until near the period of the gray dawn, this hideous drama of revivification was repeated; how each terrific relapse was only into a sterner and apparently more irredeemable death; how each agony wore the aspect of a struggle with some invisible foe; and how each struggle was succeeded by I know not what of wild change in the personal appearance of the corpse? Let me hurry to the conclusion.

The greater part of the fearful night had worn away, and she who had been dead once again stirred — and now more vigorously than hitherto, although arousing from a dissolution

more appalling in its utter hopelessness than
any. I had long ceased to struggle or to move,
and remained sitting rigidly upon the ottoman,
a helpless prey to a whirl of violent emotions,
of which extreme awe was perhaps the least terrible, the least consuming. The corpse, I repeat,
stirred, and now more vigorously than before.
The hues of life flushed up with unwonted energy into the countenance — the limbs relaxed
— and, save that the eyelids were yet pressed
heavily together, and that the bandages and
draperies of the grave still imparted their charnel character to the figure, I might have
dreamed that Rowena had indeed shaken off,
utterly, the fetters of Death. But if this idea was
not, even then, altogether adopted, I could at
least doubt no longer, when, arising from the
bed, tottering, with feeble steps, with closed
eyes, and with the manner of one bewildered in
a dream, the thing that was enshrouded advanced boldly and palpably into the middle of
the apartment.

I trembled not — I stirred not — for a crowd
of unutterable fancies connected with the air,
the stature, the demeanor, of the figure, rushing
hurriedly through my brain, had paralyzed —
had chilled me into stone. I stirred not — but
gazed upon the apparition. There was a mad
disorder in my thoughts — a tumult unappeas-
able. Could it, indeed, be the *living* Rowena
who confronted me? Could it, indeed, be
Rowena *at all* — the fair-haired, the blue-eyed

Lady Rowena Trevanion of Tremaine? Why, *why* should I doubt it? The bandage lay heavily about the mouth — but then might it not be the mouth of the breathing Lady of Tremaine? And the cheeks — there were the roses as in her noon of life — yes, these might indeed be the fair cheeks of the living Lady of Tremaine. And the chin, with its dimples, as in health, might it not be hers? — but *had she then grown taller since her malady?* What inexpressible madness seized me with that thought? One bound, and I had reached her feet! Shrinking from my touch, she let fall from her head unloosened, the ghastly cerements [34] which had confined it, and there streamed forth into the rushing atmosphere of the chamber huge masses of long and disheveled hair; *it was blacker than the raven wings of midnight!* And now slowly opened *the eyes* of the figure which stood before me. "Here then, at least," I shrieked aloud, "can I never — can I never be mistaken — these are the full, and the black, and the wild eyes — of my lost love — of the Lady — of the LADY LIGEIA."

[34] cerements — a waxed winding sheet, used in the past to wrap dead bodies.

THE MASK
OF THE RED DEATH

THE "Red Death" had long devastated the country.

No pestilence had ever been so fatal, or so hideous. Blood was its Avatar [35] and its seal — the redness and the horror of blood. There were sharp pains, and sudden dizziness, and then profuse bleeding at the pores, with dissolution. The scarlet stains upon the body and especially upon the face of the victim, were the pest ban which shut him out from the aid and from the sympathy of his fellow men. And the whole seizure,

[35] Avatar — the descent and incarnation of a deity in earthly form; taken from Hinduism. Here, Poe is saying that blood is the symbol of the plague which "took over" the country.

progress, and termination of the disease were the incidents of half an hour.

But the Prince Prospero was happy and dauntless and sagacious. When his dominions were half depopulated, he summoned to his presence a thousand hale and light-hearted friends from among the knights and dames of his court, and with these retired to the deep seclusion of one of his castellated abbeys. This was an extensive and magnificent structure, the creation of the prince's own eccentric yet august taste. A strong and lofty wall girdled it in. This wall had gates of iron. The courtiers, having entered, brought furnaces and massive hammers and welded the bolts. They resolved to leave means neither of ingress nor egress to the sudden impulses of despair or of frenzy from within. The abbey was amply provisioned. With such precautions the courtiers might bid defiance to contagion. The external world could take care of itself. In the meantime it was folly to grieve, or to think. The prince had provided all the appliances of pleasure. There were buffoons, there were improvisators, there were ballet dancers, there were musicians, there was Beauty, there was wine. All these and security were within. Without was the "Red Death."

It was toward the close of the fifth or sixth month of his seclusion, and while the pestilence raged most furiously abroad, that the Prince Prospero entertained his thousand friends at a masked ball of the most unusual magnificence.

It was a voluptuous scene, that masquerade.

But first let me tell of the rooms in which it was
held. There were seven — an imperial suite. In
many palaces, however, such suites form a long
and straight vista, while the folding doors slide
back nearly to the walls on either hand, so that
the view of the whole extent is scarcely impeded.
Here the case was very different, as might have
been expected from the duke's love of the bizarre. The apartments were so irregularly disposed that the vision embraced but little more
than one at a time. There was a sharp turn at
every twenty or thirty yards, and at each turn a
novel effect. To the right and left, in the middle
of each wall, a tall and narrow Gothic window
looked out upon a closed corridor which pursued the windings of the suite. These windows
were of stained glass whose color varied in accordance with the prevailing hue of the decorations of the chamber into which it opened. That
at the eastern extremity was hung, for example,
in blue — and vividly blue were its windows.
The second chamber was purple in its ornaments and tapestries, and here the panes were
purple. The third was green throughout, and
so were the casements. The fourth was fur-
nished and lighted with orange — the fifth with
white — the sixth with violet. The seventh apartment was closely shrouded in black-velvet tapestries that hung all over the ceiling and down
the walls, falling in heavy folds upon a carpet of
the same material and hue. But in this chamber only, the color of the windows failed to cor-
respond with the decorations. The panes here

were scarlet — a deep blood color. Now in no one of the seven apartments was there any lamp or candelabrum, amid the profusion of golden ornaments that lay scattered to and fro or depended from the roof. There was no light of any kind emanating from lamp or candle within the suite of chambers. But in the corridors that followed the suite, there stood, opposite to each window, a heavy tripod, bearing a brazier of fire, that projected its rays through the tinted glass and so glaringly illumined the room. And thus were produced a multitude of gaudy and fantastic appearances. But in the western or black chamber the effect of the firelight that streamed upon the dark hangings through the blood-tinted panes was ghastly in the extreme, and produced so wild a look upon the countenances of those who entered that there were few of the company bold enough to set foot within its precincts at all.

It was in this apartment, also, that there stood against the western wall, a gigantic clock of ebony. Its pendulum swung to and fro with a dull, heavy, monotonous clang; and when the minute hand made the circuit of the face, and the hour was to be stricken, there came from the brazen lungs of the clock a sound which was clear and loud and deep and exceedingly musical, but of so peculiar a note and emphasis that, at each lapse of an hour, the musicians of the orchestra were constrained to pause, momentarily, in their performance, to hearken to the sound; and thus the waltzers perforce ceased their evolutions; and there was a brief disconcert of the whole gay company; and, while the chimes of the clock yet rang, it was observed that the giddiest grew pale, and the more aged and sedate passed their hands over their brows as if in confused revery or meditation. But when the echoes had fully ceased, a light laughter at once prevaded the assembly; the musicians looked at each other and smiled as if at their own nervousness and folly, and made whispering vows, each to the other, that the next chiming of the clock should produce in them no similar emotion, and then, after the lapse of sixty minutes (which embrace three thousand and six hundred seconds of the Time that flies), there came yet another chiming of the clock, and then were the same disconcert and tremulousness and meditation as before.

But, in spite of these things, it was a gay and magnificent revel. The tastes of the duke were peculiar. He had a fine eye for colors and effects. He disregarded the *decora* of mere fashion. His plans were bold and fiery, and his conceptions glowed with barbaric lustre. There are some who would have thought him mad. His followers felt that he was not. It was necessary to hear and see and touch him to be *sure* that he was not.

He had directed, in great part, the movable embellishments of the seven chambers, upon occasion of this great *fête;* and it was his own guiding taste which had given character to the masqueraders. Be sure they were grotesque.

There were much glare and glitter and pi-
quancy and phantasm — much of what has been
since seen in *Hernani*.[36] There were arabesque
figures with unsuited limbs and appointments.
There were delirious fancies such as the madman fashions. There were much of the beautiful,
much of the wanton, much of the bizarre, something of the terrible, and not a little of that
which might have excited disgust. To and fro in
the seven chambers there stalked, in fact, a multitude of dreams. And these — the dreams —
writhed in and about, taking hue from the
rooms, and causing the wild music of the orchestra to seem as the echo of their steps. And, anon,
there strikes the ebony clock which stands in
the hall of the velvet. And then, for a moment,
all is still, and all is silent save the voice of the
clock. The dreams are stiff-frozen as they stand.
But the echoes of the chime die away — they
have endured but an instant — and a light, half-
subdued laughter floats after them as they depart. And now again the music swells, and the
dreams live, and writhe to and fro more merrily
than ever, taking hue from the many-tinted windows through which stream the rays from the
tripods. But to the chamber which lies most
westwardly of the seven there are now none of
the maskers who venture; for the night is wan-
ing away; and there flows a ruddier light
through the blood-colored panes; and the blackness of the sable drapery appalls; and to him
whose foot falls upon the sable carpet, there

36 *Hernani* — a poetic drama by Victor Hugo.

comes from the near clock of ebony a muffled peal more solemnly emphatic than any which reaches *their* ears who indulge in the more remote gaieties of the other apartments.

But these other apartments were densely crowded, and in them beat feverishly the heart of life. And the revel went whirlingly on, until at length there commenced the sounding of midnight upon the clock. And then the music ceased, as I have told; and the evolutions of the waltzers were quieted; and there was an uneasy cessation of all things as before. But now there were twelve strokes to be sounded by the bell of the clock; and thus it happened, perhaps, that more of thought crept, with more of time, into the meditations of the thoughtful among those who reveled. And thus too, it happened, perhaps, that before the last echoes of the last chime had utterly sunk into silence, there were many individuals in the crowd who had found leisure to become aware of the presence of a masked figure which had arrested the attention of no single individual before. And the rumor of this new presence having spread itself whisperingly around, there arose at length from the whole company a buzz, or murmur, expressive of disapprobation and surprise — then, finally, of terror, of horror, and of disgust.

In an assembly of phantasms such as I have painted, it may well be supposed that no ordinary appearance could have excited such sensation. In truth the masquerade license of the night was nearly unlimited; but the figure in

question had out-Heroded Herod, and gone beyond the bounds of even the prince's indefinite
decorum. There are chords in the hearts of the
most reckless which cannot be touched without
emotion. Even with the utterly lost, to whom
life and death are equally jests, there are matters
of which no jest can be made. The whole company, indeed, seemed now deeply to feel that in
the costume and bearing of the stranger neither
wit nor propriety existed. The figure was tall
and gaunt, and shrouded from head to foot in
the habiliments of the grave. The mask which
concealed the visage was made so nearly to re-
semble the countenance of a stiffened corpse
that the closest scrutiny must have had difficulty
in detecting the cheat. And yet all this might
have been endured, if not approved, by the mad
revelers around. But the mummer had gone so
far as to assume the type of the Red Death. His
vesture was dabbled in *blood* — and his broad
brow, with all the features of the face, was be-
sprinkled with the scarlet horror.

When the eyes of Prince Prospero fell upon
this spectral image (which, with a slow and
solemn movement, as if more fully to sustain its
role, stalked to and fro among the waltzers), he
was seen to be convulsed, in the first moment
with a strong shudder either of terror or dis-
taste; but, in the next, his brow reddened with
rage.

"Who dares," he demanded hoarsely of the
courtiers who stood near him, "who dares insult us with this blasphemous mockery? Seize

him and unmask him — that we may know whom we have to hang, at sunrise, from the battlements!"

It was in the eastern or blue chamber in which stood the Prince Prospero as he uttered these words. They rang throughout the seven rooms loudly and clearly, for the prince was a bold and robust man, and the music had become hushed at the waving of his hand.

It was in the blue room where stood the prince, with a group of pale courtiers by his side. At first, as he spoke, there was a slight rushing movement of this group in the direction of the intruder, who, at the moment, was also near at hand, and now, with deliberate and stately step, made closer approach to the speaker. But from a certain nameless awe with which the mad assumptions of the mummer had inspired the whole party, there were found none who put forth hand to seize him; so that, unimpeded, he passed within a yard of the prince's person; and, while the vast assembly, as if with one impulse, shrank from the centers of the rooms to the walls, he made his way uninterruptedly, but with the same solemn and measured step which had distinguished him from the first, through the blue chamber to the purple — through the purple to the green — through the green to the orange — through this again to the white — and even thence to the violet, ere a decided movement had been made to arrest him. It was then, however, that the Prince Prospero, maddening with rage and the shame of his own momentary cowardice, rushed hurriedly through the six chambers, while none followed him on account of a deadly terror that had seized upon all. He bore aloft a drawn dagger, and had approached, in rapid impetuosity, to within three or four feet of the retreating figure, when the latter, having attained the extremity of the velvet apartment turned suddenly and confronted his pursuer. There was a sharp cry — and the dagger dropped gleaming upon the sable carpet, upon which, instantly afterward, fell prostrate in death the Prince Prospero. Then, summoning the wild courage of despair, a throng of the revelers at once threw themselves into the black apartment, and, seizing the mummer, whose tall figure stood erect and motionless within the shadow of the ebony clock, gasped in unutterable horror at finding the grave cerement and corpselike mask, which they handled with so violent a rudeness, untenanted by any tangible form.

And now was acknowledged the presence of the Red Death. He had come like a thief in the night. And one by one dropped the revelers in the blood-bedewed halls of their revel, and died each in the despairing posture of his fall. And the life of the ebony clock went out with that of the last of the gay. And the flames of the tripods expired. And Darkness and Decay and the Red Death held illimitable dominion over all.

A DESCENT INTO
THE MAELSTROM

The ways of God in Nature, as in Providence, are
not as *our* ways; nor are the models that we frame in
any way commensurate to the vastness, profundity,
and unsearchableness of His works, *which have a
depth in them greater than the well of Democritus.*
— *Joseph Glanvill*

WE HAD now reached the summit of the lofti-
est crag. For some minutes the old man
seemed too much exhausted to speak.

"Not long ago," said he at length, "and I
could have guided you on this route as well as
the youngest of my sons; but, about three years
past, there happened to me an event such as
never happened before to mortal man — or at
least such as no man ever survived to tell of —
and the six hours of deadly terror which I then
endured have broken me, body and soul. You

194

suppose me a *very* old man — but I am not. It took less than a single day to change these hairs from jet black to white, to weaken my limbs, and to unstring my nerves, so that I tremble at the least exertion, and am frightened at a shadow. Do you know I can scarcely look over this little cliff without getting giddy?"

The "little cliff," upon whose edge he had so carelessly thrown himself down to rest that the weightier portion of his body hung over it, while he was only kept from falling by the tenure of his elbow on its extreme and slippery edge — this "little cliff" arose, a sheer unobstructed precipice of black shining rock, some fifteen or sixteen hundred feet from the world of crags beneath us. Nothing would have tempted me to be within half a dozen yards of its brink. In truth so deeply was I excited by the perilous position of my companion, that I fell at full length upon the ground, clung to the shrubs around me, and dared not even glance upward at the sky — while I struggled in vain to divest myself of the idea that the very foundations of the mountain were in danger from the fury of the winds. It was long before I could reason myself into sufficient courage to sit up and look out into the distance.

"You must get over these fancies," said the guide, "for I have brought you here that you might have the best possible view of the scene of that event I mentioned — and to tell you the whole story with the spot just under your eyes.

"We are now," he continued, in that particularizing manner which distinguished him — "we are now close upon the Norwegian coast — in the sixty-eighth degree of latitude — in the great province of Nordland — and in the dreary district of Lofoden. The mountain upon whose top we sit is Helseggen, the Cloudy. Now raise yourself up a little higher — hold on to the grass if you feel giddy — so — and look out, beyond the belt of vapor beneath us, into the sea."

I looked dizzily, and beheld a wide expanse of ocean, whose waters wore so inky a hue as to bring at once to my mind the Nubian geographer's account of the *Mare Tenebrarum*. A panorama more deplorably desolate no human imagination can conceive. To the right and left, as far as the eye could reach, there lay outstretched, like ramparts of the world, lines of horridly black and beetling cliff, whose character of gloom was but the more forcibly illustrated by the surf which reared high up against it its white and ghastly crest, howling and shrieking forever. Just opposite the promontory upon whose apex we were placed, and at a distance of some five or six miles out at sea, there was visible a small, bleak-looking island; or, more properly, its position was discernible through the wilderness of surge in which it was enveloped. About two miles nearer the land, arose another of smaller size, hideously craggy and barren, and encompassed at various intervals by a cluster of dark rocks.

The appearance of the ocean, in the space between the more distant island and the shore, had something very unusual about it. Although, at the time, so strong a gale was blowing landward that a brig in the remote offing lay to under a double-reefed trysail, and constantly plunged her whole hull out of sight, still there was here nothing like a regular swell, but only a short, quick, angry cross dashing of water in every direction — as well in the teeth of the wind as otherwise. Of foam there was little except in the immediate vicinity of the rocks.

"The island in the distance," resumed the old man, "is called by the Norwegians Vurrgh. The one midway is Moskoe. That a mile to the northward is Ambaaren. Yonder are Islesen, Hotholm, Keildhelm, Suarven, and Buckholm. Further off — between Moskoe and Vurrgh — are Otterholm, Flimen, Sandflesen, and Stockholm. These are the true names of the places — but why it has been thought necessary to name them at all, is more than either you or I can understand. Do you hear anything? Do you see any change in the water?"

We had now been about ten minutes upon the top of Helseggen, to which we had ascended from the interior of Lofoden, so that we had caught no glimpse of the sea until it had burst upon us from the summit. As the old man spoke, I became aware of a loud and gradually increasing sound, like the moaning of a vast herd of buffaloes upon an American prairie; and at the same moment I perceived that what seamen term the *chopping* character of the ocean beneath us was rapidly changing into a current which set to the eastward. Even while I gazed, this current acquired a monstrous velocity. Each moment added to its speed — to its headlong impetuosity. In five minutes the whole sea, as far as Vurrgh, was lashed into ungovernable fury; but it was between Moskoe and the coast that the main uproar held its sway. Here the vast bed of the waters, seamed and scarred into a thousand conflicting channels, burst suddenly into frenzied convulsion — heaving, boiling, hissing — gyrating in gigantic and innumerable vortices, and all whirling and plunging on to the eastward with a rapidity which water never elsewhere assumes, except in precipitous descents.

In a few minutes more, there came over the scene another radical alteration. The general surface grew somewhat more smooth, and the whirlpools, one by one, disappeared, while prodigious streaks of foam became apparent where none had been seen before. These streaks, at length, spreading out to a great distance, and entering into combination, took unto themselves the gyratory motion of the subsided vortices, and seemed to form the germ of another more vast. Suddenly — very suddenly — this assumed a distinct and definite existence, in a circle of more than a mile in diameter. The edge of the whirl was represented by a broad belt of gleaming spray; but no particle of this slipped into the mouth of the terrific funnel, whose interior, as far as the eye could fathom it, was a smooth, shining, and jet-black wall of water, inclined to the horizon at an angle of some forty-five degrees, speeding dizzily round and round with a swaying and sweltering motion, and sending forth to the winds an appalling voice, half shriek, half roar, such as not even the mighty cataract of Niagara ever lifts up in its agony to Heaven.

The mountain trembled to its very base, and the rock rocked. I threw myself upon my face, and clung to the scant herbage in an excess of nervous agitation.

"This," said I at length, to the old man — "this *can* be nothing else than the great whirlpool of the Maelström."

"So it is sometimes termed," said he. "We Norwegians call it the Moskoe-ström, from the island of Moskoe in the midway."

The ordinary account of this vortex had by no means prepared me for what I saw. That of Jonas Ramus, which is perhaps the most circumstantial of any, cannot impart the faintest conception either of the magnificence, or of the horror of the scene — or of the wild bewildering sense of *the novel* which confounds the beholder. I am not sure from what point of view the writer in question surveyed it, nor at what time; but it could neither have been from the summit of Helseggen, nor during a storm. There are some passages of his description, nevertheless, which may be quoted for their details, although their effect is exceedingly feeble in conveying an impression of the spectacle.

"Between Lofoden and Moskoe," he says, "the depth of the water is between thirty-six and forty fathoms; but on the other side, toward Ver [Vurrgh] this depth decreases so as not to afford a convenient passage for a vessel, without the risk of splitting on the rocks, which happens even in the calmest weather. When it is flood, the stream runs up the country between Lofoden and Moskoe with a boisterous rapidity; but the roar of its impetuous ebb to the sea is scarce equalled by the loudest and most dreadful cataracts; the noise being heard several leagues off, and the vortices or pits are of such an extent and depth, that if a ship comes within its attraction, it is inevitably absorbed and carried down to the bottom, and there beat to pieces against the rocks; and when the water relaxes, the fragments thereof are thrown up again. But these intervals of tranquillity are only at the turn of the ebb and flood, and in calm weather, and last but a quarter of an hour, its violence gradually returning. When the stream is most boisterous, and its fury heightened by a storm, it is dangerous to come within a Norway mile of it. Boats, yachts, and ships have been carried away by not guarding against it before they were carried within its reach. It likewise happens frequently, that whales come too near the stream, and are overpowered by its violence; and then it is impossible to describe their howlings and bellowings in their fruitless struggles to disengage themselves. A bear once, attempting to swim from Lofoden to Moskoe, was caught by the stream and borne down, while he roared terribly, so as to be heard on shore. Large stocks of firs and pine trees, after being absorbed by the current, rise again broken and torn to such a degree as if bristles grew upon them. This plainly shows the bottom to consist of craggy rocks, among which they are whirled to and fro. This stream is regulated by the flux and reflux of the sea — it being constantly high and low water every six hours. In the year 1645, early in the morning of Sexagesima Sunday,[37] it raged with such noise and impetuosity that the very stones of the houses on the coast fell to the ground."

In regard to the depth of the water, I could not see how this could have been ascertained at all in the immediate vicinity of the vortex. The "forty fathoms" must have reference only to portions of the channel close upon the shore either of Moskoe or Lofoden. The depth in the centre of the Moskoe-ström must be unmeasurably greater; and no better proof of this fact is necessary than can be obtained from even the sidelong glance into the abyss of the whirl which may be had from the highest crag of Helseggen. Looking down from this pinnacle upon the

[37] Sexagesima Sunday — the second Sunday before Lent.

howling Phlegethon below, I could not help smiling at the simplicity with which the honest Jonas Ramus records, as a matter difficult of belief, the anecdotes of the whales and the bears, for it appeared to me, in fact, a self-evident thing, that the largest ships of the line in existence, coming within the influence of that deadly attraction, could resist it as little as a feather the hurricane, and must disappear bodily and at once.

The attempts to account for the phenomenon — some of which I remember, seemed to me sufficiently plausible in perusal — now wore a very different and unsatisfactory aspect. The idea generally received is that this, as well as three smaller vortices among the Ferroe Islands, "have no other cause than the collision of waves rising and falling, at flux and reflux, against a ridge of rocks and shelves, which confines the water so that it precipitates itself like a cataract; and thus the higher the flood rises, the deeper must the fall be, and the natural result of all is a whirlpool or vortex, the prodigious suction of which is sufficiently known by lesser experiments." — These are the words of the Encyclopædia Britannica. Kircher and others imagine that in the centre of the channel of the maelström is an abyss penetrating the globe, and issuing in some very remote part — the Gulf of Bothnia being somewhat decidedly named in one instance. This opinion, idle in itself, was the one to which, as I gazed, my imagination most

readily assented; and, mentioning it to the
guide, I was rather surprised to hear him say
that, although it was the view almost universally
entertained of the subject by the Norwegians, it
nevertheless was not his own. As to the former
notion he confessed his inability to comprehend
it; and here I agreed with him — for, however
conclusive on paper, it becomes altogether un-
intelligible, and even absurd, amid the thunder
of the abyss.

"You have had a good look at the whirl now,"
said the old man, "and if you will creep round
this crag, so as to get in its lee, and deaden the
roar of the water, I will tell you a story that will
convince you I ought to know something of the
Moskoe-ström."

I placed myself as desired, and he proceeded.

"Myself and my two brothers once owned a
schooner-rigged smack of about seventy tons
burden, with which we were in the habit of
fishing among the islands beyond Moskoe,
nearly to Vurrgh. In all violent eddies at sea
there is good fishing, at proper opportunities,
if one has only the courage to attempt it; but
among the whole of the Lofoden coastmen, we
three were the only ones who made a regular
business of going out to the islands, as I tell you.
The usual grounds are a great way lower down
to the southward. There fish can be got at all
hours, without much risk, and therefore these
places are preferred. The choice spots over here
among the rocks, however, not only yield the

finest variety, but in far greater abundance; so that we often got in a single day, what the more timid of the craft could not scrape together in a week. In fact, we made it a matter of desperate speculation — the risk of life standing instead of labor, and courage answering for capital.

"We kept the smack in a cove about five miles higher up the coast than this; and it was our practice, in fine weather, to take advantage of the fifteen minutes' slack to push across the main channel of the Moskoe-ström, far above the pool, and then drop down upon anchorage somewhere near Otterholm, or Sandflesen, where the eddies are not so violent as elsewhere. Here we used to remain until nearly time for slack water again, when we weighed and made for home. We never set out upon this expedition without a steady side wind for going and coming — one that we felt sure would not fail us before our return — and we seldom made a miscalculation upon this point. Twice, during six years, we were forced to stay all night at anchor on account of a dead calm, which is a rare thing indeed just about here; and once we had to remain on the grounds nearly a week, starving to death, owing to a gale which blew up shortly after our arrival, and made the channel too boisterous to be thought of. Upon this occasion we should have been driven out to sea in spite of everything (for the whirlpools threw us round and round so violently, that, at length, we fouled our anchor and dragged it), if it had not been that we drifted into one of the innumerable cross currents — here today and gone tomorrow — which drove us under the lee of Flimen, where, by good luck, we brought up.

"I could not tell you the twentieth part of the difficulties we encountered 'on the ground' — it is a bad spot to be in, even in good weather— but we made shift always to run the gauntlet of the Moskoe-ström itself without accident; although at times my heart has been in my mouth when we happened to be a minute or so behind or before the slack. The wind sometimes was not as strong as we thought it at starting, and then we made rather less way than we could wish, while the current rendered the smack unmanageable. My eldest brother had a son eighteen years old, and I had two stout boys of my own. These would have been of great assistance at such times, in using the sweeps as well as afterward in fishing — but, somehow, although we ran the risk ourselves, we had not the heart to let the young ones get into the danger — for, after all is said and done, it *was* a horrible danger, and that is the truth.

"It is now within a few days of three years since what I am going to tell you occurred. It was on the tenth of July, 18 — , a day which the people of this part of the world will never forget — for it was one in which blew the most terrible hurricane that ever came out of the heavens. And yet all the morning, and indeed until late in the afternoon, there was a gentle and steady breeze from the southwest, while the sun shone brightly, so that the oldest seaman among us could not have foreseen what was to follow.

"The three of us — my two brothers and myself — had crossed over to the islands about two o'clock P.M., and soon nearly loaded the smack with fine fish, which, we all remarked, were more plenty that day than we had ever known them. It was just seven, *by my watch,* when we weighed and started for home, so as to make the worst of the Ström at slack water, which we knew would be at eight.

"We set out with a fresh wind on our starboard quarter, and for some time spanked along at a great rate, never dreaming of danger, for indeed we saw not the slightest reason to apprehend it. All at once we were taken aback by a breeze from over Helseggen. This was most unusual — something that had never happened to us before — and I began to feel a little uneasy, without exactly knowing why. We put the boat on the wind, but could make no headway at all for the eddies, and I was upon the point of proposing to return to the anchorage, when, looking astern, we saw the whole horizon covered with a singular copper-colored cloud that rose with the most amazing velocity.

"In the meantime the breeze that had headed us off fell away and we were dead becalmed, drifting about in every direction. This state of things, however, did not last long enough to give us time to think about it. In less than a minute the storm was upon us — in less than two the sky was entirely overcast — and what with this and the driving spray, it became suddenly so dark that we could not see each other in the smack.

"Such a hurricane as then blew it is folly to attempt describing. The oldest seaman in Norway never experienced anything like it. We had let our sails go by the run before it cleverly took us; but, at the first puff, both our masts went by the board as if they had been sawed off — the mainmast taking with it my youngest brother, who had lashed himself to it for safety.

"Our boat was the lightest feather of a thing that ever sat upon water. It had a complete flush deck, with only a small hatch near the bow, and this hatch it had always been our custom to batten down when about to cross the Ström, by way of precaution against the chopping seas. But for this circumstance we should have foundered at once — for we lay entirely buried for some moments. How my elder brother escaped destruction I cannot say, for I never had an opportunity of ascertaining. For my part, as soon as I had let the foresail run, I threw myself flat on deck, with my feet against the narrow gunwale of the bow, and with my hands grasping a ring-bolt near the foot of the foremast. It was mere instinct that prompted me to do this — which was undoubtedly the very best thing I could have done — for I was too much flurried to think.

"For some moments we were completely deluged, as I say, and all this time I held my breath, and clung to the bolt. When I could stand it no longer I raised myself upon my knees, still keeping hold with my hands, and thus got my head clear. Presently our little boat gave herself a shake, just as a dog does in coming out of the water, and thus rid herself, in some measure, of the seas. I was now trying to get the better of the stupor that had come over me, and to collect my senses so as to see what was to be done, when I felt somebody grasp my arm. It was my elder brother, and my heart leaped for joy, for I had been sure that he was overboard — but the next moment all this joy was turned into horror — for he put his mouth close to my ear, and screamed out the word *'Moskoe-ström!'*

"No one ever will know what my feelings were at that moment. I shook from head to foot as if I had had the most violent fit of ague. I knew what he meant by that one word well enough — I knew what he wished to make me understand. With the wind that now drove us on, we were bound for the whirl of the Ström, and nothing could save us!

"You perceive that in crossing the Ström *channel,* we always went a long way up above the whirl, even in the calmest weather, and then had to wait and watch carefully for the slack — but now we were driving right upon the pool itself, and in such a hurricane as this! 'To be sure,' I thought, 'we shall get there just about the slack — there is some little hope in that' —

but in the next moment I cursed myself for being so great a fool as to dream of hope at all. I knew very well that we were doomed, had we been ten times a ninety-gun ship.

"By this time the first fury of the tempest had spent itself, or perhaps we did not feel it so much, as we scudded before it, but at all events the seas, which at first had been kept down by the wind, and lay flat and frothing, now got up into absolute mountains. A singular change, too, had come over the heavens. Around in every direction it was still as black as pitch, but nearly overhead there burst out, all at once, a circular rift of clear sky — as clear as I ever saw — and of a deep bright blue — and through it there blazed forth the full moon with a lustre that I never before knew her to wear. She lit up everything about us with the greatest distinctness — but, oh God, what a scene it was to light up!

"I now made one or two attempts to speak to my brother — but in some manner which I could not understand, the din had so increased that I could not make him hear a single word, although I screamed at the top of my voice in his ear. Presently he shook his head, looking as pale as death, and held up one of his fingers, as if to say, 'listen!'

"At first I could not make out what he meant — but soon a hideous thought flashed upon me. I dragged my watch from its fob. It was not going. I glanced at its face by the moonlight, and then burst into tears as I flung it far away into the ocean. *It had run down at seven o'clock! We were behind the time of the slack, and the whirl of the Ström was in full fury!*

"When a boat is well built, properly trimmed, and not deep laden, the waves in a strong gale, when she is going large, seem always to slip from beneath her — which appears strange to a landsman — and this is what is called *riding*, in sea phrase.

"Well, so far we had ridden the swells very cleverly; but presently a gigantic sea happened to take us right under the counter, and bore us with it as it rose — up — up — as if into the sky. I would not have believed that any wave could rise so high. And then down we came with a sweep, a slide, and a plunge that made me feel sick and dizzy, as if I was falling from some lofty mountaintop in a dream. But while we were up I had thrown a quick glance around — and that one glance was all-sufficient. I saw our exact position in an instant. The Moskoe-ström whirlpool was about a quarter of a mile dead ahead — but no more like the everyday Moskoeström than the whirl, as you now see it, is like a mill-race. If I had not known where we were, and what we had to expect, I should not have recognized the place at all. As it was, I involuntarily closed my eyes in horror. The lids clenched themselves together as if in a spasm.

"It could not have been more than two minutes afterward until we suddenly felt the waves subside, and were enveloped in foam. The boat made a sharp half turn to larboard, and then shot off in its new direction like a thunderbolt. At the same moment the roaring noise of the water was completely drowned in a kind of shrill shriek — such a sound as you might imagine given out by the waterpipes of many thousand steam vessels letting off their steam all together. We were now in the belt of surf that always surrounds the whirl; and I thought, of course, that another moment would plunge us into the abyss, down which we could only see indistinctly on account of the amazing velocity with which we were borne along. The boat did not seem to sink into the water at all, but to skim like an air bubble upon the surface of the surge. Her starboard side was next the whirl, and on the larboard arose the world of ocean we had left. It stood like a huge writhing wall between us and the horizon.

"It may appear strange, but now, when we were in the very jaws of the gulf, I felt more composed than when we were only approaching it. Having made up my mind to hope no more, I got rid of a great deal of that terror which unmanned me at first. I supposed it was despair that strung my nerves.

"It may look like boasting — but what I tell you is truth — I began to reflect how magnificent a thing it was to die in such a manner, and how foolish it was in me to think of so paltry a consideration as my own individual life, in view of so wonderful a manifestation of God's power. I do believe that I blushed with shame when this idea crossed my mind. After a little while I became possessed with the keenest curiosity about the whirl itself. I positively felt a *wish* to explore its depths, even at the sacrifice I was going to make; and my principal grief was that I should never be able to tell my old companions on shore about the mysteries I should see. These, no doubt, were singular fancies to occupy a man's mind in such extremity — and I have often thought since, that the revolutions of the boat around the pool might have rendered me a little light-headed.

"There was another circumstance which tended to restore my self-possession; and this was the cessation of the wind, which could not reach us in our present situation — for, as you saw for yourself, the belt of the surf is considerably lower than the general bed of the ocean, and this latter now towered above us, a high, black, mountainous ridge. If you have never been at sea in a heavy gale, you can form no idea of the confusion of mind occasioned by the wind and spray together. They blind, deafen, and strangle you, and take away all power of action or reflection. But we were now, in a great measure, rid of these annoyances — just as death-condemned felons in prison are allowed petty indulgences, forbidden them while their doom is yet uncertain.

"How often we made the circuit of the belt

it is impossible to say. We careered round and round for perhaps an hour, flying rather than floating, getting gradually more and more into the middle of the surge, and then nearer and nearer to its horrible inner edge. All this time I had never let go of the ring-bolt. My brother was at the stern, holding on to a small empty water-cask which had been securely lashed under the coop of the counter, and was the only thing on deck that had not been swept overboard when the gale first took us. As we approached the brink of the pit he let go his hold upon this, and made for the ring, from which, in the agony of his terror, he endeavored to force my hands, as it was not large enough to afford us both a secure grasp. I never felt deeper grief than when I saw him attempt this act — although I knew he was a madman when he did it — a raving maniac through sheer fright. I did not care, however, to contest the point with him. I knew it could make no difference whether either of us held on at all; so I let him have the bolt, and went astern to the cask. This there was no great difficulty in doing; for the smack flew round steadily enough, and upon an even keel — only swaying to and fro with the immense sweeps and swelters of the whirl. Scarcely had I secured myself in my new position, when we gave a wild lurch to starboard, and rushed headlong into the abyss. I muttered a hurried prayer to God, and thought all was over.

"As I felt the sickening sweep of the descent,

I had instinctively tightened my hold upon the barrel, and closed my eyes. For some seconds I dared not open them — while I expected instant destruction, and wondered that I was not already in my death-struggles with the water. But moment after moment elapsed. I still lived. The sense of falling had ceased; and the motion of the vessel seemed much as it had been before, while in the belt of foam, with the exception that she now lay more along. I took courage and looked once again upon the scene.

"Never shall I forget the sensation of awe, horror, and admiration with which I gazed about me. The boat appeared to be hanging, as if by magic, midway down, upon the interior surface of a funnel vast in circumference, prodigious in depth, and whose perfectly smooth sides might have been mistaken for ebony, but for the bewildering rapidity with which they spun around, and for the gleaming and ghastly radiance they shot forth, as the rays of the full moon, from that circular rift amid the clouds which I have already described, streamed in a flood of golden glory along the black walls, and far away down into the inmost recesses of the abyss.

"At first I was too much confused to observe anything accurately. The general burst of terrific grandeur was all that I beheld. When I recovered myself a little, however, my gaze fell instinctively downward. In this direction I was able to obtain an unobstructed view, from the manner in which the smack hung on the inclined surface of the pool. She was quite upon an even keel — that is to say, her deck lay in a plane parallel with that of the water — but this latter sloped at an angle of more than forty-five degrees, so that we seemed to be lying upon our beam-ends. I could not help observing, nevertheless, that I had scarcely more difficulty in maintaining my hold and footing in this situation, than if we had been upon a dead level; and this, I suppose, was owing to the speed at which we revolved.

"The rays of the moon seemed to search the very bottom of the profound gulf; but still I could make out nothing distinctly on account of a thick mist in which everything there was enveloped, and over which there hung a magnificent rainbow, like that narrow and tottering bridge which Mussulmen say is the only pathway between Time and Eternity. This mist, or spray, was no doubt occasioned by the clashing of the great walls of the funnel, as they all met together at the bottom — but the yell that went up to the Heavens from out of that mist I dare not attempt to describe.

"Our first slide into the abyss itself, from the belt of foam above, had carried us to a great distance down the slope; but our farther descent was by no means proportionate. Round and round we swept — not with any uniform movement — but in dizzying swings and jerks, that sent us sometimes only a few hundred yards

— sometimes nearly the complete circuit of the whirl. Our progress downward, at each revolution, was slow, but very perceptible.

"Looking about me upon the wide waste of liquid ebony on which we were thus borne, I perceived that our boat was not the only object in the embrace of the whirl. Both above and below us were visible fragments of vessels, large masses of building-timber and trunks of trees, with many smaller articles, such as pieces of house furniture, broken boxes, barrels, and staves. I have already described the unnatural curiosity which had taken the place of my original terrors. It appeared to grow upon me as I drew nearer and nearer to my dreadful doom. I now began to watch, with a strange interest, the numerous things that floated in our company. I *must* have been delirious, for I even sought *amusement* in speculating upon the relative velocities of their several descents toward the foam below. 'This fir-tree,' I found myself at one time saying, 'will certainly be the next thing that takes the awful plunge and disappears,' — and then I was disappointed to find that the wreck of a Dutch merchant ship overtook it and went down before. At length, after making several guesses of this nature, and being deceived in all — this fact — the fact of my invariable miscalculation, set me upon a train of reflection that made my limbs again tremble, and my heart beat heavily once more.

"It was not a new terror that thus affected me,

but the dawn of a more exciting *hope*. This hope arose partly from memory and partly from present observation. I called to mind the great variety of buoyant matter that strewed the coast of Lofoden, having been absorbed and then thrown forth by the Moskoe-ström. By far the greater number of the articles were shattered in the most extraordinary way — so chafed and roughened as to have the appearance of being stuck full of splinters — but then I distinctly recollected that there were *some* of them which were not disfigured at all. Now I could not account for this difference except by supposing that the roughened fragments were the only ones which had been *completely absorbed* — that the others had entered the whirl at so late a period of the tide, or, from some reason, had descended so slowly after entering, that they did not reach the bottom before the turn of the flood came, or of the ebb, as the case might be. I conceived it possible, in either instance, that they might thus be whirled up again to the level of the ocean, without undergoing the fate of those which had been drawn in earlier or absorbed more rapidly. I made, also, three important observations. The first was, that as a general rule, the larger the bodies were, the more rapid their descent — the second, that, between two masses of equal extent, the one spherical, and the other *of any other shape,* the superiority in speed of descent was with the sphere — the third, that, between two masses of equal size, the one cylindrical, and the other of any other shape, the cylinder was absorbed the more slowly. Since my escape, I have had several conversations on this subject with an old schoolmaster of the district; and it was from him that I learned the use of the words 'cylinder' and 'sphere.' He explained to me — although I have forgotten the explanation — how what I observed was, in fact, the natural consequence of the forms of the floating fragments — and showed me how it happened that a cylinder, swimming in a vortex, offered more resistance to its suction, and was drawn in with greater difficulty than an equally bulky body, of any form whatever.

"There was one startling circumstance which went a great way in enforcing these observations, and rendering me anxious to turn them to account, and this was that, at every revolution, we passed something like a barrel, or else the yard or the mast of a vessel, while many of these things, which had been on our level when I first opened my eyes upon the wonders of the whirlpool, were now high up above us, and seemed to have moved but little from their original station.

"I no longer hesitated what to do. I resolved to lash myself securely to the water cask upon which I now held, to cut it loose from the counter, and to throw myself with it into the water. I attracted my brother's attention by signs, pointed to the floating barrels that came near us, and did everything in my power to make him understand what I was about to do. I thought at length that he comprehended my design — but, whether this was the case or not, he shook his head despairingly, and refused to move from his station by the ring-bolt. It was impossible to reach him; the emergency admitted of no delay; and so, with a bitter struggle, I resigned him to his fate, fastened myself to the cask by means of the lashings which secured it to the counter, and precipitated myself with it into the sea, without another moment's hesitation.

"The result was precisely what I had hoped it might be. As it is myself who now tell you this tale — as you see that I *did* escape — and as you are already in possession of the mode in which this escape was effected, and must therefore anticipate all that I have farther to say — I will bring my story quickly to conclusion. It might have been an hour, or thereabout, after my quitting the smack, when, having descended to a vast distance beneath me, it made three or four wild gyrations in rapid succession, and, bearing my loved brother with it, plunged headlong, at once and forever, into the chaos of foam below. The barrel to which I was attached sunk very little farther than half the distance between the bottom of the gulf and the spot at which I leaped overboard, before a great change took place in the character of the whirlpool. The slope of the sides of the vast funnel became

momentarily less and less steep. The gyrations
of the whirl grew, gradually, less and less violent. By degrees, the froth and the rainbow disappeared, and the bottom of the gulf seemed
slowly to uprise. The sky was clear, the winds
had gone down, and the full moon was setting ra-
diantly in the west, when I found myself on the
surface of the ocean, in full view of the shores of
Lofoden, and above the spot where the pool
of the Moskoe-ström *had been*. It was the hour
of the slack — but the sea still heaved in mountainous waves from the effects of the hurricane.
I was borne violently into the channel of the
Ström, and in a few minutes, was hurried down
the coast into the 'grounds' of the fishermen. A
boat picked me up — exhausted from fatigue —
and (now that the danger was removed) speech-
less from the memory of its horror. Those
who drew me on board were my old mates and
daily companions — but they knew me no more
than they would have known a traveller from
the spiritland. My hair, which had been raven
black the day before, was as white as you see it
now. They say too that the whole expression of
my countenance had changed. I told them my
story — they did not believe it. I now tell it to
you — and I can scarcely expect you to put more
faith in it than did the merry fishermen of
Lofoden."

THE IMP OF
THE PERVERSE

IN THE consideration of the faculties and impulses — of the *prima mobilia* of the human soul — the phrenologists have failed to make room for a propensity which, although obviously existing as a radical, primitive, irreducible sentiment, has been equally overlooked by all the moralists who have preceded them. In the pure arrogance of the reason, we have all overlooked it. We have suffered its existence to escape our senses, solely through want of belief — of faith — whether it be faith in Revelation, or faith in the Kabbala. The idea of it has never occurred to us, simply because of its supererogation. We saw no *need* of the impulse — for the prosperity. We could not perceive its necessity. We could not understand, that is to say, we could not have understood, had the notion of this *primum mobile* ever obtruded itself; we could not have understood in what manner it might be made to further the objects of humanity, either temporal or eternal. It çannot be denied that phrenology and, in great measure, all metaphysicianism have been concocted a priori. The intellectual or logical man, rather than the understanding or observant man, set himself to imagine designs — to dictate purposes to God. Having thus fathomed, to his satisfaction, the intentions of Jehovah, out of these intentions he built his innumerable systems of mind. In the matter of phrenology, for example, we first determined, naturally enough, that it was the design of the Deity that man should eat. We then assigned to man an organ of alimentiveness, and this organ is the scourge with which the Deity compels man, will-I nill-I, into eating. Secondly, having settled it to be God's will that man should continue his species, we discovered an organ of amativeness, forthwith. And so with combativeness, with ideality, with causality, with constructiveness — so, in short, with every organ, whether representing a propensity, a moral sentiment, or a faculty of the pure intellect. And in these arrangements of the principia of human action, the Spurzheimites, whether right or wrong, in part or upon the whole, have but followed, in principle, the footsteps of their predecessors: deducing and establishing everything from the preconceived destiny of man, and upon the ground of the objects of his Creator.

It would have been wiser, it would have been safer, to classify (if classify we must) upon the basis of what man usually or occasionally did, and was always occasionally doing, rather than upon the basis of what we took it for granted the Deity intended him to do. If we cannot comprehend God in his visible works, how then in his inconceivable thoughts, that call the works into being? If we cannot understand him in his objective creatures, how then in his substantive moods and phases of creation?

Induction, a posteriori, would have brought phrenology to admit, as an innate, and primitive principle of human action, a paradoxical something, which we may call *perverseness*, for want of a more characteristic term. In the sense I intend, it is, in fact, a *mobile* without motive, a motive not motiviert. Through its promptings we act without comprehensible object; or, if this shall be understood as a contradiction in terms, we may so far modify the proposition as to say that through its promptings we act, for the reason that we should *not*. In theory, no reason can be more unreasonable; but, in fact, there is none more strong. With certain minds, under certain conditions, it becomes absolutely irresistible. I am not more certain that I breathe than that the assurance of the wrong or error of any action is often the one unconquerable *force* which impels us, and alone impels us to its prosecution. Nor will this overwhelming tendency to do wrong for the wrong's sake admit of analysis, or resolution into ulterior elements. It is a radical, a primitive impulse — elementary. It will be said, I am aware, that when we persist in acts because we feel we should *not* persist in them, our conduct is but a modification of that which ordinarily springs from the *combativeness* of phrenology. But a glance will show the fallacy of this idea. The phrenological combativeness has for its essence the necessity of self-defense. It is our safeguard against injury. Its principle regards our well-being; and thus the desire to be well is excited simultaneously with its development. It follows that the desire to be well must be excited simultaneously with any principle which shall be merely a modification of combativeness; but in the case of that something which I term *perverseness,* the desire to be well is not only not aroused, but a strongly antagonistical sentiment exists.

An appeal to one's own heart is, after all, the best reply to the sophistry just noticed. No one who trustingly consults and thoroughly questions his own soul will be disposed to deny the entire radicalness of the propensity in question. It is not more incomprehensible than distinctive. There lives no man who at some period has not been tormented, for example, by an earnest desire to tantalize a listener by circumlocution. The speaker is aware that he displeases; he has every intention to please; he is usually curt, precise, and clear; the most laconic and luminous language is struggling for utterance upon his tongue; it is only with difficulty that he restrains himself from giving it flow; he dreads and deprecates the anger of him whom he addresses; yet, the thought strikes him, that by certain involutions and parentheses this anger may be engendered. That single thought is enough. The impulse increases to a wish, the wish to a desire, the desire to an uncontrollable longing, and the longing (to the deep regret and mortification of the speaker, and in defiance of all consequences) is indulged.

We have a task before us which must be speedily performed. We know that it will be ruinous to make delay. The most important crisis of our life calls, trumpet-tongued, for immediate energy and action. We glow, we are consumed with eagerness to commence the work, with the anticipation of whose glorious result our whole souls are on fire. It must, it shall be undertaken today, and yet we put if off until tomorrow; and why? There is no answer, except that we feel *perverse,* using the word with no comprehension of the principle. Tomorrow arrives, and with it a more impatient anxiety to do our duty; but with this very increase of anxiety arrives, also, a nameless, a positively fearful, because unfathomable, craving for delay. This craving gathers strength as the moments fly. The last hour for action is at hand. We tremble with the violence of the conflict within us, of the definite with the indefinite, of the substance with the shadow. But, if the contest has proceeded thus far, it is the shadow which pervails — we struggle in vain. The clock strikes, and is the knell of our welfare. At the same time, it is the chanticleer note to the ghost that has so long overawed us. It flies — it disappears — we are free. The old energy returns. We will labor *now.* Alas, it is *too late!*

We stand upon the brink of a precipice. We peer into the abyss — we grow sick and dizzy. Our first impulse is to shrink from the danger. Unaccountably we remain. By slow degrees our sickness and dizziness and horror become merged in a cloud of unnamable feeling. By gradations, still more imperceptible, this cloud assumes shape, as did the vapor from the bottle out of which arose the genii in the *Arabian Nights*. But out of this *our* cloud upon the precipice's edge, there grows into palpability, a shape, far more terrible than any genii or any demon of a tale, and yet it is but a thought, although a fearful one, and one which chills the very marrow of our bones with the fierceness of the delight of its horror. It is merely the idea of what would be our sensations during the sweeping precipitancy of a fall from such a height. And this fall, this rushing annihilation, for the very reason that it involves that one most ghastly and loathsome of all the most ghastly and loathsome images of death and suffering which have ever presented themselves to our imagination — for this very cause do we now the most vividly desire it. And because our reason violently deters us from the brink, *therefore* do we the most impetuously approach it. There is no passion in nature so demoniacally impatient as that of him who, shuddering upon the edge of a precipice, thus meditates a plunge. To indulge, for a moment, in any attempt at *thought*, is to be inevitably lost; for reflection but urges us to forbear, and *therefore* it is, I say, that we *cannot.* If there be no friendly arm to check us, or if we fail in a sudden effort to prostrate ourselves backward from the abyss, we plunge, and are destroyed.

Examine these and similar actions as we will, we shall find them resulting solely from the spirit of the *Perverse.* We perpetrate them merely because we feel that we should *not.* Beyond or behind this there is no intelligible principle; and we might, indeed, deem this perverseness a direct instigation of the archfiend, were it not occasionally known to operate in furtherance of good.

I have said thus much, that in some measure I may answer your question — that I may explain to you why I am here — that I may assign to you something that shall have at least the faint aspect of a cause for my wearing these fetters, and for my tenanting this cell of the condemned. Had I not been thus prolix, you might either have misunderstood me altogether, or, with the rabble, have fancied me mad. As it is, you will easily perceive that I am one of the many uncounted victims of the Imp of the Perverse.

It is impossible that any deed could have been wrought with a more thorough deliberation. For weeks, for months, I pondered upon the means of the murder. I rejected a thousand schemes, because their accomplishment involved a *chance* of detection. At length, in reading some French memoirs, I found an account of a nearly fatal illness that occurred to Madame

Pilau, through the agency of a candle acciden-
tally poisoned. The idea struck my fancy at once.
I knew my victim's habit of reading in bed. I
knew, too, that his apartment was narrow and
ill-ventilated. But I need not vex you with im-
pertinent details. I need not describe the easy
artifices by which I substituted, in his bedroom
candle stand, a wax light of my own making for
the one which I there found. The next morning
he was discovered dead in his bed, and the
coroner's verdict was: "Death by the visitation
of God."

Having inherited his estate, all went well
with me for years. The idea of detection never
once entered my brain. Of the remains of the
fatal taper I had myself carefully disposed. I had
left no shadow of a clue by which it would be
possible to convict, or even to suspect, me of the
crime. It is inconceivable how rich a sentiment
of satisfaction arose in my bosom as I reflected
upon my absolute security. For a very long period of time I was accustomed to revel in this
sentiment. It afforded me more real delight
than all the mere worldly advantages accruing
from my sin. But there arrived at length an
epoch, from which the pleasurable feeling grew,
by scarcely perceptible gradations, into a haunt-
ing and harassing thought. It harassed because
it haunted. I could scarcely get rid of it for an
instant. It is quite a common thing to be thus
annoyed with the ringing in our ears, or rather
in our memories, of the burden of some ordinary song, or some unimpressive snatches from

an opera. Nor will we be the less tormented if the song in itself be good, or the opera air meritorious. In this manner, at last, I would perpetually catch myself pondering upon my security, and repeating, in a low undertone, the phrase, "I am safe."

One day, while sauntering along the streets, I arrested myself in the act of murmuring, half aloud these customary syllables. In a fit of petulance, I remodelled them thus: "I am safe — I am safe — yes — if I be not fool enough to make open confession!"

No sooner had I spoken these words than I felt an icy chill creep to my heart. I had had some experience in these fits of perversity (whose nature I have been at some trouble to explain), and I remembered well that in no instance had I successfully resisted their attacks. And now my own casual self-suggestion, that I might possibly be fool enough to confess the murder of which I had been guilty, confronted me, as if the very ghost of him whom I had murdered — and beckoned me on to death.

At first, I made an effort to shake off this nightmare of the soul. I walked vigorously — faster — at length I ran. I felt a maddening desire to shriek aloud. Every succeeding wave of thought overwhelmed me with new terror, for, alas! I well, too well, understood that to *think*, in my situation, was to be lost. I still quickened my pace. I bounded like a madman through the crowded thoroughfares. At length, the populace took the alarm and pursued me. I felt *then* the consummation of my fate. Could I have torn out my tongue, I would have done it; but a rough voice resounded in my ears — a rougher grasp seized me by the shoulder. I turned — I gasped for breath. For a moment I experienced all the pangs of suffocation; I became blind, and deaf, and giddy; and then some invisible fiend, I thought, struck me with his broad palm upon the back. The long-imprisoned secret burst forth from my soul.

They say that I spoke with a distinct enunciation, but with marked emphasis and passionate hurry, as if in dread of interruption before concluding the brief but pregnant sentences that consigned me to the hangman and to hell.

Having related all that was necessary for the fullest judicial conviction, I fell prostrate in a swoon.

But why shall I say more? Today I wear these chains, and am *here!* Tomorrow I shall be fetterless! — *but where?*

POEMS

TO HELEN [38]

Helen, thy beauty is to me
  Like those Nicean barks of yore,
That gently, o'er a perfumed sea,
  The weary, way-worn wanderer bore
  To his own native shore.

On desperate seas long wont to roam,
  Thy hyacinth hair, thy classic face,
Thy Naiad [39] airs have brought me home
  To the glory that was Greece
And the grandeur that was Rome.

Lo! in yon brilliant window-niche
  How statuelike I see thee stand!
  The agate lamp within thy hand,
Ah! Psyche,[40] from the regions which
  Are Holy Land!

---

38 Helen — although this poem was not written to Helen
of Troy (beautiful wife of Menelaus, whose abduction by
Paris brought about the Trojan war), Poe's imagery
implies the comparison.
39 Naiad — a water nymph of Greek mythology, who lived
in lakes, rivers, streams, or fountains and gave life to them.
40 Psyche — Roman mythological princess loved by Cupid.

ELDORADO [41]

GAILY bedight,
A gallant knight,
In sunshine and in shadow,
Had journeyed long,
Singing a song,
In search of Eldorado.

But he grew old —
This knight so bold—
And o'er his heart a shadow
Fell as he found
No spot of ground
That looked like Eldorado.

And, as his strength
Failed him at length,
He met a pilgrim shadow—
"Shadow," said he,
"Where can it be—
This land of Eldorado?"

"Over the Mountains
Of the Moon,
Down the Valley of the Shadow,
Ride, boldly ride,"
The shade replied,
"If you seek for Eldorado!"

41 Eldorado — a city or country of fabulous riches, reputed
by 16-century explorers to have existed in South America.
The name has come to mean any place of wealth,
abundance, or opportunity.

THE RAVEN

ONCE upon a midnight dreary, while I pondered, weak and weary,
Over many a quaint and curious volume of
forgotten lore —
While I nodded, nearly napping, suddenly there
came a tapping,
As of some one gently rapping, rapping at my
chamber door.
" 'Tis some visitor," I muttered, "tapping at my
chamber door —
Only this and nothing more."

Ah, distinctly I remember it was in the bleak
December,
And each separate dying ember wrought its
ghost upon the floor.
Eagerly I wished the morrow — vainly I had
sought to borrow
From my books surcease of sorrow — sorrow for
the lost Lenore —
For the rare and radiant maiden whom the
angels name Lenore —
Nameless here for evermore.

And the silken sad uncertain rustling of each
purple curtain
Thrilled me — filled me with fantastic terrors
never felt before;

So that now, to still the beating of my heart, I
    stood repeating:
" 'Tis some visitor entreating entrance at my
    chamber door —
Some late visitor entreating entrance at my
    chamber door;
                This it is and nothing more."

Presently my soul grew stronger; hesitating then
    no longer,
"Sir," said I, "or Madam, truly your forgiveness
    I implore;
But the fact is I was napping, and so gently you
    came rapping,
And so faintly you came tapping, tapping at my
    chamber door,
That I scarce was sure I heard you" — here I
    opened wide the door —
                Darkness there and nothing more.

Deep into the darkness peering, long I stood
    there wondering, fearing,
Doubting, dreaming dreams no mortals ever
    dared to dream before;
But the silence was unbroken, and the stillness
    gave no token,
And the only word there spoken was the
    whispered word, "Lenore!"
This I whispered, and an echo murmured back
    the word, "Lenore!" —
                Merely this and nothing more.

Back into the chamber turning, all my soul
within me burning,
Soon again I heard a tapping something louder
than before.
"Surely," said I, "surely that is something at my
window lattice;
Let me see, then, what thereat is, and this
mystery explore —
Let my heart be still a moment, and this mystery
explore —
                'Tis the wind and nothing more."

Open here I flung the shutter, when, with many
a flirt and flutter,
In there stepped a stately Raven of the saintly
days of yore.
Not the least obeisance made he; not a minute
stopped or stayed he,
But, with mien of lord or lady, perched above
my chamber door —
Perched upon a bust of Pallas [42] just above my
chamber door —
                Perched, and sat, and nothing more.

Then this ebony bird beguiling my sad fancy
into smiling,
By the grave and stern decorum of the counte-
nance it wore,
"Though thy crest be shorn and shaven, thou,"
I said, "art sure no craven,

[42] Pallas — Usually Pallas Athena, Greek goddess of wisdom
and women's crafts.

Ghastly grim and ancient Raven wandering
   from the Nightly shore —
Tell me what thy lordly name is on the Night's
   Plutonian [43] shore!"
           Quoth the Raven, "Nevermore."

Much I marvelled this ungainly fowl to hear
   discourse so plainly,
Though its answer little meaning — little rele-
   vancy bore;
For we cannot help agreeing that no living
   human being
Ever yet was blessed with seeing bird above his
   chamber door —
Bird or beast upon the sculptured bust above
   his chamber door,
           With such name as "Nevermore."

But the Raven, sitting lonely on that placid
   bust, spoke only
That one word, as if his soul in that one word
   he did outpour.
Nothing farther then he uttered; not a feather
   then he fluttered —
Till I scarcely more than muttered: "Other
   friends have flown before —
On the morrow *he* will leave me as my Hopes
   have flown before."
           Then the bird said, "Nevermore."

[43] Plutonian — taken from Pluto, the Roman god of the
dead and of the lower world.

Startled at the stillness broken by reply so aptly
   spoken,
"Doubtless," said I, "what it utters is its only
   stock and store,
Caught from some unhappy master whom un-
   merciful Disaster
Followed fast and followed faster till his songs
   one burden bore —
Till the dirges of his Hope that melancholy
   burden bore
               Of Never — nevermore."

But the Raven still beguiling all my sad soul
   into smiling,
Straight I wheeled a cushioned seat in front of
   bird and bust and door;
Then, upon the velvet sinking, I betook myself to linking
Fancy unto fancy, thinking what this ominous
   bird of yore —
What this grim, ungainly, ghastly, gaunt, and
   ominous bird of yore
            Meant in croaking "Nevermore."

This I sat engaged in guessing, but no syllable
   expressing
To the fowl whose fiery eyes now burned into
   my bosom's core;
This and more I sat divining, with my head at
   ease reclining
On the cushion's velvet lining that the lamplight gloated o'er,

But whose velvet violet lining with the lamp-
    light gloating o'er
               She shall press, ah, nevermore!

Then, methought, the air grew denser, per-
    fumed from an unseen censer
Swung by Seraphim whose footfalls tinkled on
    the tufted floor.
"Wretch," I cried, "thy God hath lent thee —
    by these angels he hath sent thee
Respite — respite and nepenthe [44] from thy mem-
    ories of Lenore!
Quaff, oh quaff this kind nepenthe and forget
    this lost Lenore!"
               Quoth the Raven, "Nevermore."

"Prophet!" said I, "thing of evil! — prophet
    still, if bird or devil! —
Whether Tempter sent, or whether tempest
    tossed thee here ashore,
Desolate, yet all undaunted, on this desert land
    enchanted —
On this home by Horror haunted — tell me
    truly, I implore —
Is there — *is* there balm in Gilead [45]? — tell me —
    tell me, I implore!"
               Quoth the Raven, "Nevermore."

[44] nepenthe — the banishment of pain and sorrow. It is
actually a potion or drug used by the ancients to cause
forgetfulness and held by some to be opium or hashish.
[45] Gilead — a mountainous region in Jordan. Poe's question, "*is* there balm in Gilead" is a direct reference to the
hymn, which states: "There is a balm in Gilead to make
the wounded whole/There is a balm in Gilead to cleanse
the sin sick soul."

"Prophet!" said I, "thing of evil!—prophet
    still, if bird or devil!
By that heaven that bends above us—by that
    God we both adore—
Tell this soul with sorrow laden if, within the
    distant Aidenn,
It shall clasp a sainted maiden whom the angels
    name Lenore—
Clasp a rare and radiant maiden whom the
    angels name Lenore."
                    Quoth the Raven, "Nevermore."

"Be that word our sign of parting, bird or
    fiend!" I shrieked, upstarting—
"Get thee back into the tempest and the Night's
    Plutonian shore!
Leave no black plume as a token of that lie thy
    soul hath spoken!
Leave my loneliness unbroken!—quit the bust
    above my door!
Take thy beak from out my heart, and take thy
    form from off my door!"
                    Quoth the Raven, "Nevermore."

And the Raven, never flitting, still is sitting,
    still is sitting
On the pallid bust of Pallas just above my
    chamber door;
And his eyes have all the seeming of a demon's
    that is dreaming,

And the lamplight o'er him streaming throws
  his shadow on the floor;
And my soul from out that shadow that lies
  floating on the floor
                Shall be lifted — nevermore!

SONNET—TO SCIENCE

SCIENCE! true daughter of Old Time thou art!
  Who alterest all things with thy peering eyes.
Why preyest thou thus upon the poet's heart,
  Vulture, whose wings are dull realities?
How should he love thee? or how deem thee
    wise?
  Who wouldst not leave him in his wandering
To seek for treasure in the jewelled skies,
  Albeit he soared with an undaunted wing?
Hast thou not dragged Diana [46] from her car?
  And driven the Hamadryad [47] from the wood
To seek a shelter in some happier star?
  Hast thou not torn the Naiad from her flood,
The Elfin from the green grass, and from me
  The summer dream beneath the tamarind [48]
    tree?

---

[46] Diana — Roman goddess of the moon, wild animals, and
hunting.
[47] Hamadryad — a wood nymph; also a large venomous
snake of southeastern Asia and the Phillipines.
[48] tamarind — a tropical tree with hard yellow fruit and
red-striped yellow flowers.

ULALUME

THE skies they were ashen and sober;
    The leaves they were crisped and sere —
    The leaves they were withering and sere;
It was night in the lonesome October
    Of my most immemorial year;
It was hard by the dim lake of Auber,
    In the misty mid region of Weir —
It was down by the dank tarn of Auber,
    In the ghoul-haunted woodland of Weir.

Here once, through an alley Titanic,
    Of cypress, I roamed with my Soul —
    Of cypress, with Psyche, my Soul.
These were days when my heart was volcanic
    As the scoriac rivers that roll —
    As the lavas that restlessly roll
Their sulphurous currents down Yaanek
    In the ultimate climes of the pole —
That groan as they roll down Mount Yaanek
    In the realms of the boreal pole.

Our talk had been serious and sober,
    But our thoughts they were palsied and
        sere —
    Our memories were treacherous and sere —

For we knew not the month was October,
    And we marked not the night of the year
    (Ah, night of all nights in the year!) —
We noted not the dim lake of Auber
    (Though once we had journeyed down
        here) —
Remembered not the dank tarn of Auber,
    Nor the ghoul-haunted woodland of Weir.

And now, as the night was senescent
    And star-dials pointed to morn —
    As the star-dials hinted of morn —
At the end of our path a liquescent
    And nebulous lustre was born,
Out of which a miraculous crescent
    Arose with a duplicate horn —
Astarte's bediamonded crescent
    Distinct with its duplicate horn.
And I said: "She is warmer than Dian:
    She rolls through an ether of sighs —
    She revels in a region of sighs:

She has seen that the tears are not dry on
    These cheeks, where the worm never dies,
And has come past the stars of the Lion
    To point us the path to the skies —
    To the Lethean [49] peace of the skies —
Come up, in despite of the Lion,
    To shine on us with her bright eyes —
Come up through the lair of the Lion,
    With love in her luminous eyes."

[49] Lethean — Lethe, in Greek mythology, is a river in Hades which is supposed to cause forgetfulness in those who drink from it.

But Psyche, uplifting her finger,
>Said: "Sadly this star I mistrust —
>Her pallor I strangely mistrust —
Oh, hasten! — oh, let us not linger!
>Oh, fly! — let us fly! — for we must."
In terror she spoke, letting sink her
>Wings until they trailed in the dust —
In agony sobbed, letting sink her
>Plumes till they trailed in the dust —
>Till they sorrowfully trailed in the dust.

I replied: "This is nothing but dreaming:
>Let us on by this tremulous light!
>Let us bathe in this crystalline light!
Its Sybilic splendor is beaming
>With Hope and in Beauty tonight! —
>See! — it flickers up the sky through the
>night!
Ah, we safely may trust to its gleaming,
>And be sure it will lead us aright —
We safely may trust to a gleaming,
>That cannot but guide us aright,
>Since it flickers up to Heaven through the
>night."

Thus I pacified Psyche and kissed her,
>And tempted her out of her gloom —
>And conquered her scruples and gloom;
And we passed to the end of the vista,
>But were stopped by the door of a tomb —
>By the door of a legended tomb;

And I said: "What is written, sweet sister,
   On the door of this legended tomb?"
   She replied: "Ulalume — Ulalume —
   'Tis the vault of thy lost Ulalume!"

Then my heart it grew ashen and sober
   As the leaves that were crisped and sere —
   As the leaves that were withering and sere,
And I cried: "It was surely October
   On *this* very night of last year
   That I journeyed — I journeyed down
      here —
   That I brought a dread burden down
      here —
   On this night of all nights in the year,
   Ah, what demon has tempted me here?
Well I know, now, this dim lake of Auber —
   This misty mid region of Weir —
Well I know, now, this dank tarn of Auber,
   This ghoul-haunted woodland of Weir."

THE BELLS

I

HEAR the sledges with the bells —
Silver bells!
What a world of merriment their melody
foretells!
How they tinkle, tinkle, tinkle,
In the icy air of night!
While the stars that oversprinkle
All the heavens seem to twinkle
With a crystalline delight;
Keeping time, time, time,
In a sort of Runic rhyme,
To the tintinnabulation that so musically
wells
From the bells, bells, bells, bells,
Bells, bells, bells —
From the jingling and the tinkling of the bells.

II

Hear the mellow wedding bells,
Golden bells!
What a world of happiness their harmony
foretells!
Through the balmy air of night

How they ring out their delight!
From the molten-golden notes,
And all in tune,
What a liquid ditty floats
To the turtle-dove that listens, while she gloats
On the moon!
Oh, from out the sounding cells
What a gush of euphony voluminously wells!
How it swells!
How it dwells
On the Future! how it tells
Of the rapture that impels
To the swinging and the ringing
Of the bells, bells, bells,
Of the bells, bells, bells, bells,
Bells, bells, bells —
To the rhyming and the chiming of the bells!

III

Hear the loud alarum bells —
Brazen bells!
What a tale of terror, now, their turbulency
tells!
In the startled ear of night
How they scream out their affright!
Too much horrified to speak,
They can only shriek, shriek,
Out of tune,
In a clamorous appealing to the mercy of
the fire,
In a mad expostulation with the deaf and
frantic fire,

Leaping higher, higher, higher,
With a desperate desire,
And a resolute endeavor
Now — now to sit, or never,
By the side of the pale-faced moon.
Oh, the bells, bells, bells!
What a tale their terror tells
Of despair!
How they clang, and clash, and roar!
What a horror they outpour
On the bosom of the palpitating air!
Yet the ear it fully knows,
By the twanging,
And the clanging,
How the danger ebbs and flows;
Yet the ear distinctly tells,
In the jangling,
And the wrangling,
How the danger sinks and swells,
By the sinking or the swelling in the anger
of the bells —
Of the bells —
Of the bells, bells, bells, bells,
Bells, bells, bells —
In the clamor and the clangor of the bells!

IV

Hear the tolling of the bells —
Iron bells!
What a world of solemn thought their melody
compels!

In the silence of the night,
How we shiver with affright
At the melancholy menace of their tone!
For every sound that floats
From the rust within their throats
Is a groan.
And the people — ah, the people —
They that dwell up in the steeple,
All alone,
And who tolling, tolling, tolling,
In that muffled monotone,
Feel a glory in so rolling
On the human heart a stone —
They are neither man nor woman —
They are neither brute nor human —
They are Ghouls:
And their king it is who tolls;
And he rolls, rolls, rolls,
Rolls
A pæan from the bells!
And his merry bosom swells
With the pæan of the bells!
And he dances, and he yells;
Keeping time, time, time,
In a sort of Runic rhyme,
To the pæan of the bells —
Of the bells:
Keeping time, time, time,
In a sort of Runic rhyme,
To the throbbing of the bells —
Of the bells, bells, bells —
To the sobbing of the bells;

Keeping time, time, time,
As he knells, knells, knells,
In a happy Runic rhyme,
To the rolling of the bells —
Of the bells, bells, bells —
To the tolling of the bells,
Of the bells, bells, bells, bells —
Bells, bells, bells —
To the moaning and the groaning of the bells.

ANNABEL LEE

It was many and many a year ago,
 In a kingdom by the sea,
That a maiden there lived whom you may know
 By the name of Annabel Lee;
And this maiden she lived with no other
  thought
 Than to love and be loved by me.

I was a child and *she* was a child,
 In this kingdom by the sea:
But we loved with a love that was more than
  love —
 I and my Annabel Lee;
With a love that the winged seraphs of heaven
 Coveted her and me.

And this was the reason that, long ago,
 In this kingdom by the sea,
A wind blew out of a cloud, chilling
 My beautiful Annabel Lee;
So that her high-born kinsman came
 And bore her away from me,
To shut her up in a sepulchre
 In this kingdom by the sea.

The angels, not half so happy in heaven,
  Went envying her and me —
Yes! — that was the reason (as all men know,
  In this kingdom by the sea)
That the wind came out of the cloud by night,
  Chilling and killing my ANNABEL LEE.

But our love it was stronger by far than the love
  Of those who were older than we —
  Of many far wiser than we —
And neither the angels in heaven above,
  Nor the demons down under the sea,
Can ever dissever my soul from the soul
  Of the beautiful ANNABEL LEE,

For the moon never beams, without bringing
   me dreams
  Of the beautiful ANNABEL LEE;
And the stars never rise, but I feel the bright
   eyes
  Of the beautiful ANNABEL LEE;
And so, all the night-tide, I lie down by the side
Of my darling — my darling — my life and my
   bride,
  In the sepulchre there by the sea,
  In her tomb by the sounding sea.

A SELECTIVE BIBLIOGRAPHY

Books about Poe are scarce, as are editions of his work. This list includes the most readily available collection of Poe's work, the standard biography, and a paperback collection of critical essays.

The Complete Tales and Poems of Edgar Allan Poe, edited by Hervey Allen. New York, Modern Library, 1938.

Edgar Allan Poe: *A Critical Biography,* by Arthur Hobson Quinn. New York, D. Appleton-Century Company, 1941.

Poe: *A Collection of Critical Essays,* edited by Robert Regan. (Twentieth Century Views.) Englewood Cliffs, New Jersey, Prentice-Hall, Inc., 1967.